Thanksgiving in Sweetwater County

Ciara Knight

Also by Ciara Knight

The Neumarian Chronicles
Weighted
Escapement
Pendulum
Balance

Battle For Souls
Rise From Darkness
Fall From Grace
Ascension of Evil

Sweetwater County Series
Winter
Spring
Summer
Fall
Christmas
Valentines
4th of July
Thanksgiving

Riverbend
Coming in 2016:
In All My Wishes
In All My Years
In All my Life
In All My Dreams

The Shrouded Kingdoms
The Curse of Gremdon
The Secrets of Dargon (January 2016)
The Runes of Bramon (late 2016)

A Prospector's Novel
Fools Rush

An American Mail-Order Bride
Adelaide: Bride of Maryland

www.ciaraknight.com

Thanksgiving in Sweetwater County – Sweetwater County Series
Ciara Knight
ISBN-13: 978-1-939081-60-5

Cover Art: Robin Ludwig
Editor: Cora Artz

This is a work of fiction. Names, characters, places and incidents either are the product of the author's imagination or are used fictitiously. Any resemblance to actual persons, living or dead, events or locales is entirely coincidental.

Praise and Awards

USA Today Bestselling Author
Semi-finalist in the Amazon Breakthrough Novel Contest
RONE Award Finalist
LASR Book of the Month

"Wow! My first read by Ciara Knight and all I can think of is wow!"
~Night Owl Top Pick.

"Knight does a fantastic job keeping readers intrigued throughout..."
~RT Book Reviews, 4 Stars

CHAPTER ONE

Welcome to Sweetwater County, Tennessee.
Where your heart and home belong.
Population 5,000.

"More like, where your heart and home were smashed into bits," Jenna Greyson grumbled and gripped the steering wheel to keep straight on the winding road, a road leading to the past. She pulled off for a second in front of the cemetery and thought about visiting her father. A visit was long overdue, more than ten years overdue, but one glance in the rearview mirror at her sleeping daughter kept her firmly planted in the driver's seat.

The tall gradual hill, with brown grass and dotted with yellow and orange flowers, looked peaceful, a good resting place for a great man. She sniffled. Even today the hole in her heart remained.

Hearing her cell phone ring, she pushed the button on the console and abandoned her moment of sorrow for the new life ahead. "Hello?"

"I need to know where my grey suit is," Shane said,

his voice as stern and unforgiving as the day she'd left him. Not because he was brokenhearted she'd divorced him. No, she was sure now he'd never really cared for her. He was only bitter she dared to walk out on him without permission.

"In case you forgot, I'm no longer your wife." Jenna glanced back at Sadie. To her relief, her four-year-old remained soundly asleep in her car seat.

"Yes, well, my ex-wife packed all my stuff up while I was at work, so I have no idea which box has what in it."

Jenna sighed. Sighed for their failed marriage. Sighed for her daughter growing up without a father. Sighed for the epic mistake she was about to make by returning home to Creekside and her mother. "I waited a month for you to pack your stuff. The house sold. I had no choice. All the boxes are labeled. Your suit would be in the one marked *suits*."

Shane huffed. "Fine. Where are my golf clubs? And don't tell me in a box labeled *golf clubs* because they're not."

"Oh, golf clubs? I don't know where your prized golf clubs are. I'm not sure I remember what they even look like. I think I saw them about as much as I saw you over the last four years." Jenna made a quick check in the rearview mirror to make sure Sadie still couldn't hear them squabble. During all the mess of their divorce, that was the one thing Jenna tried to do, keep Sadie from the ugliness.

"I told you I'd be home more. I offered to make this work. You're the one who left and filed divorce papers."

“You only agreed to stay home if I sent Sadie away.”

“That’s not fair,” Shane said, his tone deepening. “We can’t care for Sadie, you know that. She needs special help. I offered to put her in a place that could deal with her.”

Fire heated her skin and threatened to erupt from her ears. “Deal with her? You think she's a dog?”

“Stop twisting my words. Deal with her needs. She can’t talk. She can’t learn. She can’t even use the bathroom and she’s four years old. She’ll never be normal. I know, I grew up next door to a boy who was retarded.”

That word rolled around her mind, slammed against her skull, ricochet down her throat, and plummeted to her stomach, causing a large splash of stinging acid to rise up in protest. “Don’t ever call my child that again. She is a beautiful child, who just has some learning difficulties.”

“Grammaticism doesn’t change that she’s disabled.”

Again, she thought she’d explode with four years of pent up anger and resentment. “This conversation is over. Find your own precious golf clubs, and don’t ever call me again. Papers are signed, divorce is final. You should be happy. You took everything except my car and clothes.”

“You gave me everything and ran,” Shane shot back.

“It was that or stay married to you for years as you squabbled over material things that don’t matter. Every time we argued, it upset Sadie, and unlike you I care what happens to my daughter."

"Someday you'll realize I was right, but by then it'll be too late. You'll be putting Sadie in a home, and you'll be without a husband. Goodbye, Jenna."

The phone disconnected. Her pulse knocked repeatedly in her brain as if to warn her of the validity of his words, but love conquered all. Perhaps not the happily-ever-after marriage kind, but the mother-daughter kind did.

She took several cleansing breaths, knowing that Sadie would notice her agitation the moment she woke if she didn't calm down. The green-eyed, strawberry-blonde little thing didn't just look like an angel, Jenna swore she had some kind of cosmic power to sense things. That, and math. Why did Shane never see her gifts, only her challenges?

The road curved around by an old printing shop and déjà vu hit again like a head-on collision. How was she going to face everyone after running off the moment she graduated high school to get her degree, marry some big shot, and have a family only to return home broken and lost? It didn't matter. This wasn't about her, not anymore. This was about what was best for Sadie. Scoring the job as the director of the Center for Autism was best for Sadie. There would be a roof over their heads and she would be able to spend all day with Sadie until she started kindergarten next year. Not to mention, she could finally use the degree that she'd worked so hard to earn all those years ago.

On the corner, she spotted an old home, the one

that she'd been told about. A sharp turn to the left and she pulled into the driveway. A swing set to the right, white front porch, large yard. Perfect. It even appeared as if the home had been restored. Pale green latticework decorated the peak of the roof. It looked like an old-fashioned schoolhouse, all it needed was a bell. She felt her lips curve into a smile. How long had it been since she'd smiled?

"Mama?"

Jenna spun in her seat. "Yes, hon?"

"Home?"

"Yes, we're home, darling." Jenna unbuckled her seat belt and opened her door to the cool November mountain air. She'd always loved this time of year. If Creekside was good for something, it was for celebrating the holidays. Everything in town would be lit up soon. Even now, there would be hay and straw, scarecrows and pumpkins, and best of all the Thanksgiving Feast. It was a town social event that everyone attended. Even the sick and elderly were bussed to the event. There was always love in this town. It just wasn't the love she wanted.

If only Drew Walker hadn't broken her heart, she would've stayed in Creekside. What would he look like now? Same dark hair and white smile that made women melt? Or was he balding and fat after ten years?

"Mama, out?"

She shook off the memories and slid her hand under the buckle to undo Sadie's restraints. By age one, Jenna had to turn the buckle backwards because Sadie would hit it with a toy until it released. She had to be a descendent of Houdini. She was one epic escape artist.

"Come on, baby. Let's go check out our new home." She set Sadie down on her feet, but kept a good hold of her hand.

"Home." She pointed once more and giggled.

"You like it?"

Sadie nodded three times. It was always three times. Then she walked on her tiptoes up the stairs to the front porch.

As promised, Jenna found the key under the mat and opened the front door. Hardwood floors ran the length of the house, white crown molding and large baseboards framing each room. Whoever refurbished the place did an amazing job.

They took a few steps inside. Off the entry was the front room, the perfect size for a classroom with enough space for computers. She could put up all sorts of colorful teaching posters and wall hangings. To the left, she discovered another room of equal size that would fit a few tables and chairs, just what the children would need for lunchtime and art projects. Straight ahead, some stairs led up to the second floor, where Sadie and she were to live. In the back of the home was a smaller room off a quaint kitchen. Luckily the appliances were included. She couldn't afford those right now, even with the money Shane sent monthly for mandatory child support.

Heading back toward the front of the house, they found a small bathroom in the hall with a tub, sink, and toilet. It would work fine for the school.

"Room?" Sadie pointed to the stairs.

"You want to check out where your new bedroom will be?"

She nodded three times then tiptoed to the stairs and up to the second floor. The house smelled faintly of fresh paint and floor stain. The upstairs looked similar to the main floor. The only thing the rooms needed was paint, their clothes hung up, some necessary supplies, and they'd be home. Maybe she'd upgrade the furniture someday, but for now it was perfect.

Sadie broke free from Jenna's hand and raced from room to room, until she settled on one. "Pink!" It was the room in the front of the home, which she'd always preferred.

"You want to paint your room pink?"

Three nods.

"Sure, we can paint it pink. We'll have to paint the other rooms, too."

"Pink!" Everything had to be pink. Except food. Food should never be pink in Sadie's world.

"We'll see." Jenna made her way to the master bedroom and found the larger room was equipped with its own bath. The claw foot tub welcomed her with its smooth, white surface, promising a muscle soothing, warm bath. It had been two days since her last shower. They'd been on the road nonstop, and she didn't like taking her eyes off Sadie in a hotel room.

"Would you like to play dolls?"

Three nods.

"Okay, wait here. I'm going to unload the car, and I'll get your dolls. You can play right here in my new room on the bed, okay?"

Three nods.

Jenna ran downstairs, out the door, grabbed a couple of boxes, and darted back upstairs to check on Sadie. She was rolling back and forth on the mattress giggling, feet in the air and tossing a pillow up and down. Jenna set the boxes in the corner and made five more trips until the car was empty. Locating the box labeled *Sadie's toys,* Jenna rummaged through it and found her dolls.

"Okay, sweetie. You're going to stay right here and play, right?"

Three nods.

Just to be safe, Jenna closed and locked the bedroom door then stacked two boxes in front of it before she entered the bathroom. The cool white tile chilled her feet. She turned on the water and enjoyed the warmth on her hands. "Can you count by fives for Mommy?" she called through the open door.

"Five, ten, fifteen, twenty..."

Her voice softened, so Jenna leaned back to check. To her relief, Sadie was still counting while brushing her doll's hair.

The water poured out of the faucet and steam rose in the bathroom. She retrieved a towel from the box labeled *linens*, patted Sadie on the head, and returned to the bathroom.

By the time, she shut off the water, Sadie had grown tired of the counting game and was lost in the world of her dolls. After one more check on her, Jenna undressed and climbed into the hot water. It coated her skin with therapeutic bliss. Her muscles relaxed and she closed her eyes, freeing her mind of the last several days—her argument with Shane, the long drive, the judging looks she knew were coming—and focusing on the future she would build for Sadie and herself.

Heeeef, Heeeef, Heeef. Klaplunk.

"Sadie? Sadie? What's that noise? Sadie?"

A fresh coat of fear painted her body. She hopped from the tub, slipping and sliding on wet tile. Her feet lost traction and she flew back, her head hitting the side of the tub. Grey haze seeped into her vision, but she shook her head and crawled to the edge of the bathroom. She peered out into the room and discovered only an open door and an overturned box.

Sadie was gone.

CHAPTER TWO

"Deputy Walker, you're going out with us Saturday night," Sheriff Jimmy Mason ordered from the other end of the phone.

Drew settled into his seat, placed his cup of coffee in the holder, and revved his cruiser. "Is that an order from my boss?"

"No, from Trianna, my wife. Lord knows she's the boss and you don't want to make her mad."

Judy and James Benjamin passed hand in hand, walking along the sidewalk of downtown Creekside. It was difficult to believe they'd reunited after so many years. He'd left his prominent job as head of psychology at the Veteran's Administration Hospital in Miami to return to his high school sweetheart. He took Judy's arm, and helped her up the sidewalk since she wore her usual tailored dress and high heels. James wore his usual slacks and a button up. They always looked well put together and ready for customers. It was hard to believe James worked on their farm most days. They both nodded in greeting and smiled before entering J&L Antiques.

"I'm not feeling it, man. Jessica wasn't my type

back in high school, and she isn't my type now."

"You mean she doesn't live up to the *Jenna standard*," Jimmy said, his tone dropping from playful to lecturing.

Drew tapped the window button and clicked his seatbelt into place. Crisp air blew through his cruiser with a warning of a chilly conversation. "That was old a decade ago, and it's even older now. Give it a rest."

"I'll give it a rest when you own up to it and move on. You're not getting any younger, you know. You'll lose that girlish figure of yours and then who will have you? Can't be the playboy of Sweetwater County forever. Younger and better lookin' is gonna take over that rep."

"Ha. Ha. So funny. Just 'cause that wife of yours has you in an apron all the time doesn't mean I want to join the reform school for bachelors. Stop watching all those chick shows on TV and play your man card once in a while. The answer's *no* to couples night and *no* to any more set ups, okay?" Drew adjusted his rearview mirror. "I've gotta head out to the veteran's facility and take a statement about the vandalism."

"Don't forget to drop off those supplies at the new Center for Autism," Jimmy said.

Drew shoved the car into reverse. "You got it. If no one's there, I'll drop it on the front porch."

Jimmy cleared his throat in that I-know-something-I'm-not-sharing way. "Someone'll be there. Make sure you knock and give it to the new facility admin."

Before Drew could ask what was up, Jimmy ended

the call. He would've dialed back, but knew that if Sheriff Mason had some sort of top secret intel, he was better off finding out on his own. Of course, top secret usually meant a town squabble or a county board vote, neither of which Drew wanted anything to do with. That was for the town sheriff to handle and that's why he preferred being a deputy.

He eyed the beautiful decorations of scarecrows, bales of hay, and happy faces on his way past the Main Street shops. He loved his hometown, but he tended to stay out of the business of others as much as possible. It only made life complicated.

At the edge of town, he did a drive-by of the abandoned building at the end of the block to check for mischievous teens and any squatters that might have made their way to town. Determining all was clear, he found his way back to Main and down the long hill out of town.

Around the curve, he turned onto a side street. Something darted into the road. A girl, a little girl. He slammed his foot hard on the brake and cut his wheel sharply to the left. His cruiser squealed to a stop, the two right wheels on the curb, two left on the street.

His heart rapid-fired in his chest. He couldn't see the small child beyond his hood. Did he hit her? No, he would've heard a thump or felt his tires rumbled underneath. The thought flipped his stomach inside out. He swallowed the roaring of fear and steadied his hands. Nothing ever got him this panicked. Not even being shot at in the army, or on the job. But a kid, kids were different.

He managed to find his footing on the asphalt and peer around the front fender of his car. There she was, a little girl with wispy goldish-red hair and a tiny frame. She rocked with her hands over her ears, humming. He squatted by her side. “Hey, you okay?”

The child only hummed louder, rocked harder, and covered her ears tighter.

“Sadie! Sadie, where are you?” A woman’s voice cried from the nearby yard. Not just any woman’s voice, her voice. After all these years, it was as clear and crisp as if a yesterday memory instead of a long distance one. Jenna Mitchell. The girl who’d stolen his heart, his everything, then disappeared without a word.

“Mama, Mama, Mama,” the young girl mumbled.

“Sadie?” he asked.

“Mama, Mama, Mama.” She lowered her doll-sized hands and glimpsed at him with huge green eyes, eyes the color of an emerald. Eyes that belonged to only one other in the world. Jenna.

“Is that your mama calling you?”

She tilted her porcelain perfect face then nodded three times.

“Can I take your hand? We should get out of the road, and your mama must be worried.” Drew held out his hand and she slipped her tiny fingers into his palm. He took a long breath, settled his insides, and readied himself to face the one woman he'd ever loved.

Sadie twisted her legs underneath her and stood no taller than the hood of his car. She walked on her tiptoes to the curb where she clung to his wrist with both hands and swung up to the grass.

"Sadie!" Jenna's voice cracked with emotion and she raced across the lawn with only a towel wrapped around her body. He tried to force his eyes away, but her beauty was just as intoxicating as it was in high school. Same full lips, nice curves, and strawberry blonde hair. She skidded to a halt on her knees and flung her arms around Sadie. "I told you to stay right there. You scared Mommy."

She hadn't seen him. She hadn't realized she was half-dressed and outside on her front lawn. She had found her little girl.

"Thank you, officer. Thank you so much." Jenna checked over her daughter, investigating each arm, each leg, her cheeks, and forehead before she looked up at him. Her bottom jaw fell and her gaze fixed on him as if scanning her phone directory for the right name. Had she forgotten about him?

"Drew," she whispered.

"Mama, Mama, Mama," Sadie repeated.

Drew shifted gears and grabbed hold of his training. "Your daughter's okay. We best get you inside, ma'am."

She shook her head and looked down. "Oh, um, yes." She swept Sadie into her arms, stood and raced barefoot up the front porch steps. Drew moved his cruiser into the driveway while still struggling to maintain his composure. It was his job to serve and protect the residents of Creekside, and it appeared as if that now included Jenna. *Mason, that scoundrel.* That was why he'd brought up her name again. He knew she was here. Boss or no boss, he'd drop kick him first chance he got.

With his chin high, his shoulders back, and his pulse racing faster than a high-speed chase, he marched up the front steps and knocked on the open front door. “Excuse me, but I thought I'd check on you both before I go.”

“We're okay.” Jenna stood next to an unpacked box, clutching the towel tight around her body. “I'm sorry, I thought Sadie would remain in the house while I took a quick bath, but I guess I was wrong.”

“Ah, we've got a runner here.” Drew smiled down at Sadie who nodded.

The child was adorable, but acted a little younger than she looked. It appeared as if she still wore diapers, but shouldn't she be out of them by this age? Of course, what did he know? He'd never had kids, or even been around little kids much.

“You have no idea. I can't sleep or shower because I'm scared she'll run off and get hurt. I plan to install an alarm system, but we just arrived.” Jenna shook her head, her far-off gaze smothering his need to attack her for answers. Why she ran off all those years ago? What had he done?

“Why don't you call your mother? I'm sure she'd be happy to watch her while you take a break, or your husband.” Okay, that last part slipped out, but still, he waited for her reply.

Silence sounded in the room like an early warning system.

“She doesn't know I'm in town yet.”

Drew analyzed Jenna's face then her ring finger.

Her soft lips twitched, the way they did when she was under stress, and her ringless hands fidgeted with the towel. "She also doesn't know I'm divorced. I'd appreciate it if you gave me a chance to face her before you let her know I'm here."

"It's a small town, and your mother—"

"Knows everything about everyone in every way. Yes, I know."

The way she said it sounded like there was some secret message behind it, but he didn't have the code to figure it out. He never had.

"What are you doing here, Jenna?" he asked. His words sounded more harsh and accusatory than he'd meant them to, but he needed to know why she was demolishing his wall of protection with her move to town.

"Trust me, I don't want to be in Creekside."

"Then why are you here?"

"For Sadie. After the divorce, I needed a job that I could do but still spend time with her, and Judy Benjamin convinced me it would be a perfect fit. Not that I owe you an explanation, Drew Walker." Her tone switched from sad to angry in a single breath. "I'm allowed to live in the town I grew up in. I have just as much right as you do."

"You left your hometown without a word, so playing that card isn't gonna sit well with some people in town."

"Some people? Or you, Drew? Listen, I don't care who you married, knocked-up, or are having an affair with. Go about your business. Sadie and I aren't here to interrupt your life. I'm just trying to make a better life for my daughter." She stomped to the front door. "Now, if you'll excuse me." She stood at the door and tapped her foot.

"I think I'm long past due for an explanation, but it can wait." He turned to Sadie. "It was nice to meet you." He smiled at her.

Sadie waved backwards and giggled. "Bye, bye, bye."

"If you need anything else, ma'am, I'm sure Sheriff Mason will be happy to assist you." He left Sadie sitting on the floor next to the unpacked box. Left Jenna standing in her towel at the front door, but didn't leave his heart this time. It had been in a ten-year coma.

CHAPTER THREE

All night Jenna tossed and turned, one hand on Sadie's shoulder to make sure she still slept and the other on her chest keeping her heart from breaking all over again.

Sadie's tiny fingers drew circles on her lower back. Somehow, her daughter always knew when she needed a little TLC.

Jenna rolled over, forcing a smile and the energy to get out of bed to face her new life. One without the comforts of a well-to-do husband, without the distance from her mother, and without the delusion that she didn't care about Drew Walker, and his ultimate betrayal, since the day she'd left Creekside. She'd thought the pain had mended over the years, but the thin sutures securing the gaping hole in her heart had burst, spilling the hurt all over again.

"Mama, Mama, Mama. Morning." Sadie clapped and kissed Jenna's cheek.

Shaking off the debilitating memory of Drew and Jessica in an intimate embrace under an oak tree, she decided it was time to face today. "Want to go to town? I need to visit someone. You might remember her. She met you briefly a few months ago. She's your grandmother."

"Bye, bye, bye?"

Jenna smiled and tucked Sadie's thin hair behind her ear. "Yes, we can go bye-bye."

In only a few minutes, Sadie dressed herself in a frilly blue dress and handed her hairbrush to Jenna. With each stroke, Sadie nearly fell asleep. The child loved the feeling of physical contact to the point where her eyes rolled back in her head. Shane hated it, always yelling for Sadie to sit right and stop looking stupid. Jenna only hoped the scars of his words wouldn't be permanent. Someday, Sadie would show the world how gifted and smart she truly was.

After several hundred strokes, Jenna left Sadie to play dolls and dressed herself. "Do you want a treat while we're out? I thought we could get something special to celebrate us moving here."

"Ice cream?"

Jenna slipped her green long-sleeve turtleneck over her head, ignoring the nagging memory that Drew had always loved her in green. He'd said it made her eyes shine across the entire county. Did he use the same words with Jessica? Jenna shook the image from her head and shoved her socked feet into her black boots.

After they brushed their teeth and got the buckles done on Sadie's white shoes, they headed down the driveway. "It's not a far walk. Would you like to go in the car or walk?"

Sadie hopped up and down. "Walk, walk, walk."

Jenna took a tight hold of her hand and led her up the street. It wouldn't be long before someone spotted her and the entire town knew she was back. She only hoped she'd reach her mother first to control the impending collateral damage. She'd been too much of a coward to tell the truth before she arrived, fearing her mother would be at her doorstep demanding she and Shane worked out their marital problems. She could have demanded all she wanted, but that would've never happened.

They reached the edge of town and Sadie squealed with delight. She tried to pull her hand away, but Jenna kept hold and squatted to eye level. "You need to listen, Sadie. If you don't behave, there'll be no ice cream and we won't be able to stay. You must keep hold of Mommy's hand."

"Aha, aha, aha." She nodded with each *Aha* and settled at Jenna's side, but continued to gently tug her toward the scarecrow at the first lamppost.

She hugged the scarecrow, but then shoved it from her and rubbed her arms. "Noooooo."

"Too stiff?" Jenna asked. She should've known her daughter wouldn't like the texture. "It's still cute to look at. We can use our eyes instead of our hands. Imagine he's guarding the town."

Sadie smiled and half-skipped, half-trotted up to the flower shop and stopped to sniff the yellow buds in the green container at the front door. After two sneezes, she skipped and trotted to the antique store. Judy's store. She'd mentioned she had gone into business with a girl named Lisa, who married her son, Eric. She wondered when Eric had returned to Creekside. He'd left for university around the same time as her brother. He'd been handsome and older, but still just her brother's friend in her eyes.

So much had changed, yet the town looked the same. They reached the coffee shop, updated at some point in the last ten years, but with the same kind of vibe. Beyond the window, she spotted Judy Gaylord Benjamin waving at them.

"We're going to stop inside here for a moment. Would you like to meet the nice lady who told Mommy about this job? She was like a second mother to me when I was growing up."

Sadie bounced. "Aha, aha, aha."

A short man she didn't recognized held the door open for them. There were many new faces, along with familiar ones in the coffee shop.

"How are you? How was your trip, darling?" Judy swept over and wrapped her welcoming arms around Jenna. The warmth and loving, strong arms from her childhood settled her nerves a smidgen.

"It was fine. We're getting settled in our new home before the school opens in a few weeks."

Judy released her then knelt gracefully, despite her heels and dress, to meet Sadie at eye level. "This beautiful girl can't be Sadie. She's too grown up to be that little girl."

"Me." Sadie twirled, holding out one side of her favorite blue dress. The one Shane had bought for a party in hopes she'd look normal, but never took her to after she had an accident. He was always embarrassed she wasn't potty trained by age two like all the other little girls.

"Well, I've seen pictures of you, but it's a pleasure to meet you now." Judy took her little hand and shook it without hesitation.

Sadie wobbled, but still executed a graceful curtsy. She'd practiced for days after watching it on a movie and deciding she wanted to be a princess.

Judy pointed to the front counter. "Can I get you something?"

"No, I'm good. I'm afraid my stomach isn't going to take much this morning."

"Ah, you haven't told Cathy yet. Oh, hon, you better get home quick. You know that woman has eyes and ears everywhere. Sometimes I think she's really a spy for the CIA and has bugs all over town."

Jenna laughed at how right she was. "I still don't know how she knew about Drew and I skipping lunch period and leaving campus in high school."

"Well, no teacher wanted to be the one that allowed something to happen to you. They were all scared of your mama. Cathy put the fear of God into everyone in town that had interaction with her kids. You can say a lot about Cathy Mitchell West, but she was one devoted mother."

Jenna nodded. "Devoted to the point of choking the life out of us. My brother and I couldn't leave town fast enough after we graduated."

Judy waved at a tall gentleman with a silver flat top. "Oh, just in time. I'd like you to meet James, my husband."

"Hello." James shook Jenna's hand, kissed Judy's cheek then squatted in front of Sadie. "Who is this pretty young lady in the fancy dress? Is this the princess of Sweetwater County?"

Sadie threw her arms around James.

"Oh, and a good hugger, too."

"Sadie, let Mr. West go. I'm sorry. She's excited you called her a princess."

James stood with Sadie in his arms. "Oh, no need to apologize. It's not every day I get a hug from a princess."

Jenna wasn't used to such a warm welcome with Sadie. She'd forgotten the family-style community she once belonged to. At one time, she'd had dreams of staying, despite her mother's meddling. She'd planned on attending Riverbend College and marrying Drew, but all that changed. Thank goodness her mother had applied to the University of Tennessee for her. If she hadn't, she would've had to watch Drew and Jessica get married and have a family together. Her chest tightened, knowing sooner or later she'd have to see them together.

"I think we better get going. If my mother hears about me being in Creekside before I tell her, she might go supernova on all of us."

"She's already going to have a fit over the board and me knowing you were hired for the job," Judy said.

"I'm sorry I put you in that position, Mrs. Benjamin."

"*Judy*, please. You were always like a daughter to me. And don't worry about Cathy, she kind of owes me one on the secret department." She laced her fingers with James's and they smiled at each other as if sharing an intimate secret.

"Well, I guess this isn't going to get any easier. Let's go see your grandmother, Sadie."

James lowered her to the ground. "Promise me you'll come visit us at the farm. We even have a pony now you can ride."

"Yeeeeees!" Sadie clapped and hopped on one foot.

"Good, it's settled." James tweaked her nose.

Sadie stood on her tiptoes, returned the gesture, and then held his imaginary nose to her chest.

They left the coffee shop and the warmth of welcoming friends, the aroma of coffee, and the safety of another building to walk down Main Street to her childhood home. It was such a stark contrast to their oversized home in Connecticut where they'd lived the last few years, surrounded by other large homes, large yards, and large attitudes.

They opened the wrought iron gate and entered the garden. It was manicured and in beautiful shape, the way it had been when she was a little girl. Fall flowers dotted the outskirts of several beds around well-sculpted bushes and grew over the edge of pots on the front porch. Fresh paint and some added rocking chairs made it feel like she'd stepped into a dream, one of a loving family. But once she told her mother she'd left her husband, the dream would end with her yelling and carrying on about ruining her life.

Inside the front window, she spotted her mother sitting at a small table with her new husband, Devon.

His salt and pepper hair made him look distinguished. He seemed like a nice man when they'd met, but she didn't know him well. The way they laughed and held each other's hands made Jenna smile. She'd never seen her mother so happy. The woman was a third the size she'd been when Jenna left Creekside, and her kitty sweatshirts had been replaced with current fashion. - Jenna hadn't recognized her when they'd visited. Perhaps her new husband would be a big enough distraction to keep her mother from meddling in her life. One could hope, even if there was a better chance of her finding a magical turkey on her front steps.

Sadie jumped to see inside. Her hair flying up and down snagged their attention. Her mother stood and covered her mouth, her eyes going wide, then she darted to the door.

"Oh my word, what are you doing here, darling? You should've told me you were coming. I would've picked you up from the airport."

Swept up in hugs, Jenna struggled to keep hold of Sadie's hand.

"And you brought that beautiful granddaughter of mine. Well, hello there, Ms. Sadie."

"Hi, hi, hi." Sadie twirled in her dress. "Boo?"

"It's blue," Jenna translated.

"Yes, I love your dress. You are the prettiest girl this side of the Mississippi." Her mother swooped Sadie into her arms and spun.

Devon joined them. "It's good to see you."

"Where's that husband of yours? Don't tell me he had to work again. Oh well, a man's gotta earn money to take care of his family."

Jenna wanted to tell her then and there that she'd divorced the man her mother had approved of, even though they'd barely talked for five minutes, but Cathy was dancing about and so happy, drawing all sorts of attention.

Devon placed a hand on Jenna's shoulder. "Come in and make yourself at home."

Jenna moved to take Sadie, but her mother held her daughter tight and wouldn't let go.

"I've got my grandbaby. I've raised a few kids of my own, you know."

Jenna stepped inside. The smell of childhood bombarded her senses, but there was a new mix. Devon's cologne and fresh cinnamon candles melded the past with the present.

"I can't believe you're here. I'm so excited. Please, oh please tell me you'll be here for the Thanksgiving Feast. I know I can't hope for Christmas, but I'll take Thanksgiving if I can. I'm sorry. I'm being too pushy, aren't I?"

Since when did her mother apologize for anything? Let alone even consider she might be out of control and taking over? Perhaps Judy was right. Devon had tamed the great Cathy Mitchell.

"Sit, relax. Can I get you anything? Oh, darling, I'm so glad you're here."

Jenna sunk into the sofa and eyed Devon, who busied himself in the kitchen as if he knew she had to tell her mother something in private. "I'm afraid you might not be so happy to see me once I tell you why I'm here."

Her mother froze midspin and set Sadie down. Her arms outstretched toward her grandmother, Sadie called, "Again, again, again."

Devon swooped in and lifted her up, providing an instant swing for her.

"Darlin', there is nothin' you could ever tell me that would make me wish you weren't here. Now, let's settle in for a little chat and you can tell me what's troubling you."

Jenna fidgeted with the hem of her shirt, crossed and uncrossed her ankles and shifted in her seat.

"Jenna Mitchell Greyson, you can tell your mama anything, but now you're scaring me. Out with it. I promise I won't be mad," Cathy said, but the thickening southern accent and higher tone warned of the exact opposite.

Jenna sighed. "Don't make promises you won't keep."

Cathy settled in by her side and took her hands to hold them tight in her lap. "I know I've been a little much over the years, but I promise I won't go mental on you. I've changed, promise. I swear, even though I only did things because I love you, I know it's your life and I shouldn't meddle in it unless I'm asked for my opinion. I promise you're safe to tell me anything."

Jenna cleared her throat and readied for battle. "Okay, I guess I'll just spit it out." After a quick glance to check on Sadie, she lifted her chin and said, "I divorced Shane and I've moved back to Creekside. I'm going to be running the Children's Center for Autism."

Her mama's face turned every shade of green then white. Only the sound of the ticking grandfather clock her great-grandfather had made, and Sadie's squeals sounded in the room.

"Mama, say something. Anything."

Her mother let go of her hands, smoothed out her long shirt and stood. "You need to go home, Jenna. You need to go home now."

CHAPTER FOUR

The long day turned into evening as Drew finished the last of his reports. Susan gathered her purse and keys and headed for the back door. "Don't forget, Jimmy's meeting you at Café Bliss."

Drew fought a snarl. "Yep, I'm looking forward to it."

"You don't fool me, but whatever." She sashayed out the door with that all-knowing secretary swagger she'd perfected before he could even reply.

What would he say anyway? He was going to meet his oldest friend so he could deck him. Jimmy wasn't stupid, that was why he hadn't come near the precinct today. The man never missed a day, yet had claimed Trianna needed him. But the whole family man speech didn't work on Drew at all.

He shot up, grabbed his stuff and headed home. He had a few minutes to change before meeting Jimmy.

The streets were more crowded than normal, but it was Friday evening and getting close to the holidays. He turned down Oakmont then into the side driveway to his apartment above the Cooper's garage. It looked depressingly lonely for some reason this evening. It had never felt that way before. He enjoyed the privacy and the cheap rent, but somehow it was different tonight.

He shoved open the car door and inhaled the aroma of fall. That hint of brisk air always made him want to go for a hike, or climb a mountain, or something. With heavy feet, he stomped up the rickety steps to his front door and opened it to an even more depressing scene. His sparse furnishings and lack of décor screamed workaholic bachelor. At least that was what the last girl said when she'd come over to see him.

He entered the bedroom and yanked open his bottom drawer for some street clothes. The ring he'd bought over a decade ago still sat it it's original box, stuffed in the corner of the drawer. He'd meant to sell it, not that it was worth much since he'd bought it his senior year of high school, but he'd never got around to taking it to a pawn shop.

He kicked the drawer closed and turned his back to the dresser. Shaking off the bitterness of bachelorhood and embracing his inner dog, he changed clothes, secured his weapon in his gun safe, and headed to Café Bliss.

Driving to the café, he couldn't help but let his imagination wonder back to his time with Jenna in high school. They'd been madly in love. Ate lunch together every day. She'd held his hand during his father's funeral, talked to him all night when his mom was drunk and couldn't face life again. She'd been there, every day since his sophomore year. They swore they'd always be together. That they'd grow up and do better than their own parents had done for them.

He passed by the large oak at the end of Main Street and spotted the heart carved into the bark with their initials. Jenna had carved that into the tree the night her daddy grounded her for leaving the school's campus to be with him. The night her mama said she'd ruin her life with a deadbeat like him.

With parking limited on Main, he left his truck at the Hatfield Inn and walked across the street to Café Bliss where he spotted Jimmy sitting at a two-man table with coffee already waiting.

He entered the café to the rich aroma of pumpkin and cinnamon. Jimmy stood and offered his hand. Drew took it and squeezed as hard as he could.

"Whoa. Okay, man. What's up with the death grip?" Jimmy rubbed his hand and sat down, a frown creasing his forehead.

"Don't even act innocent. You knew she was here. You knew it and sent me to her house with no warning, under the guise of delivering some things for the new center."

"Did you drop them off?"

"No, I forgot. But don't try to change the subject. How could you do that to me? You knew Jenna was there."

Jimmy shrugged and took a long draw from his coffee cup before he said, "Yeah, but you said you were over her, remember? It's been over ten years since you saw her last and you said you'd moved on. That you no longer had feelings for her."

"That's besides the point," Drew growled.

"So you admit you're still hung up on the girl."

Drew shook his head. "No, not on her. Not like that. It's just strange. I don't know."

"I do. You never got a real explanation. Not one beyond her mother's. You waited for four years. You worked hard at school, didn't date, nothing. You waited for her to return, but then her mama told you she'd married another man. That's when you really lost yourself."

"I didn't lose myself. What's this? An interrogation? Just so you know, I've already been warned that any man who gives up bachelorhood tries to convert the others to their misery."

"I'm not miserable. I just want to help my oldest friend. She's back and you can finally put your questions to rest. Ask her what happened. If she fell in love with someone and left, fine. If she really did feel trapped in a small town, fine. But why leave without a word, without a way to speak to her. Something never felt right to me." Jimmy did that sheriff chin scrub that always got on Drew's nerves.

"This isn't a crime you're trying to solve."

Jimmy held up both his hands. "I won't get involved any further, but I'd sure like to see my best bud move on with his life."

"Hey, I'm going out with Jessica tomorrow, all right?"

Jimmy chuckled. "Under duress."

"Yes, well, I can see why Trianna wears the gun belt in your family. She kind of scares me."

Jimmy laughed loud, filling the room with his voice. "You think? She's one tough lady, probably the strongest woman I've ever known."

Drew was happy for his friend, the way his eyes lit up every time Trianna's name was mentioned. And now, he'd be a dad soon. A hint of jealousy smacked Drew in the face. Not that he'd been looking for a family, but he'd always loved kids. That little girl, Sadie, was adorable.

"Hey, you still with me?" Jimmy asked.

"Huh? Oh, yep."

"All I'm saying is that you should confront her now that she's in town. That way you can give another girl a shot. A real shot, not the half-assed attempt you usually do."

"If you're talking about Jessica, I'll go. And I don't need answers from Jenna. None of that matters, not after all these years."

"You've known Jessica a long time. Do you like her?"

"I've been friends with her forever. We became close when that jerk who called himself our friend knocked her up and left town. Jessica's a strong woman, pretty, smart, done a great job raising her daughter on her own."

Jimmy shifted in his chair. "You've been a constant role model in her daughter's life all this time."

"Yeah, someone had to fill the gap so the abandoned dad disease wouldn't spread."

"So why haven't you hooked up after all this time?" Jimmy asked the hard questions.

Drew sighed. "Lord knows she's tried, but I never gave her a second thought that way. Maybe it's because

I value the only friend of the opposite sex I've ever had."

Jimmy's phone buzzed and the screen lit up. "Gotta run. I told Trianna I'd make it home in time for dinner. She's making something special. Let's meet at the diner tomorrow at six. Jessica was already planning on going with Trianna, so that'll be perfect. No pressure, just hanging out with friends at dinner. See what you think."

"All right, man. I'll see you tomorrow night." Drew drank some of the coffee Jimmy had bought him then decided to go for a walk. He'd always enjoyed walking through town, and the weather was perfect.

With cup in hand, he opened the door for two ladies then headed down the street toward the historic district. At the corner, he spotted Jenna and Sadie and his heart did a high dive off his ribs. He thought about ducking back into the coffee house, but based on her wide eyes and open mouth, Jenna had already seen him, too.

Come on, man. You've taken down criminals in dark alleys, shot terrorists in battle, certainly you're man enough to face an old girlfriend.

Sadie dragged her mother toward him. There was no escape. He slid his free hand in his pocket so he wouldn't fidget and greeted them at the edge of the building.

"Hi, hi, hi!" Sadie waved vigorously.

"Hi there, munchkin. How are you this evening? Looks like you're going out on the town with that pretty dress on."

"Princess." Sadie curtsied and spun once, wobbling when she reached the end of her circle.

"You sure do look like a princess." He rubbed the top of her head and she leaned into his hand like a sweet puppy.

He glanced at Jenna. Her face was white, with that battle look in her eyes. The one she always had after a fight with Cathy. Clearing buildings in Afghanistan was less dangerous than facing Cathy Mitchell's wrath.

"You okay?" he whispered.

She took a long breath. "Yeah, sure. Um, sorry. We were just headed home."

He scanned the road behind them. "You just came from Cathy and Devon's, right?"

She nodded and sighed. "Yes."

He ran his hand through his hair and leaned against the wall. "What did y'all fight about this time?"

Jenna rubbed her forehead. "I'm not even sure. All I know is my own mother doesn't want me living here. I'm starting to think she never did. I don't know. This is all so messy. Divorce. Moving back here after what happened. Sadie...Sadie?" She spun around. "Sadie."

Drew shot from the brick wall and scanned the area. He sidestepped Jenna and looked around the corner then back the other way and caught sight of pale blue material with white lace behind a car. The car backed out slowly, but the driver wouldn't be able to see her. He hurtled a bench and slid across the back of the car, pounding on the trunk before landing next to Sadie and grasping her to his chest.

"Oh my God! Sadie!" Jenna ran over, but he guided

her back to the sidewalk. A man rolled down his window.

"I'm so sorry. I didn't see her. Please tell me she's not hurt. I looked. I swear I looked."

"It wasn't your fault, Rusty. The child was behind your trunk, in a blind spot. She's fine, though."

He released Sadie into the arms of her mother whose hands trembled and bottom lip quivered.

He patted Rusty Miller on the shoulder and waved at Becca. "You two okay?"

"Yes. Again, so sorry, man."

"Wasn't your fault and all is good. Get home safe, you two."

Becca took hold of Rusty's hand. "We will. Thanks."

"It's too much. This is all too much." Jenna rocked with Sadie in her arms.

"Are you okay, Jenna?" He held her to him, the way he had whenever she needed a hug, whenever she got in a fight with her mother. The way he had the night her father died. In return, she leaned into him, the way she had when they were only kids, and it felt perfect.

"I'm okay. I know better. I shouldn't have been distracted," she said, her voice cracking.

"Bird."

He stroked Sadie's hair. "You saw a bird? I see. I tell you what. Next time, tell your mother and I bet she'll take you to see the bird. We have lots of birds around here."

"Aha, aha, aha," Sadie said.

There was something different about Sadie, but so adorable though.

"That's twice you've saved her. I don't know what to say. I wish I could repay you somehow. Nothing in this world is more important to me than Sadie."

"You can," he said, knowing he needed one thing from her.

She leaned away from him and straightened her green shirt. The color that always made her eyes shine beyond reality. "What's that?"

"You can talk to me about what happened ten years ago."

She chewed her bottom lip and toed the ground before she pushed her shoulders back and faced him. "If you want to, that's fine. I need to get Sadie home, though. It's time for her bath and bed. She needs to keep a strict schedule."

"Okay, how about Sunday morning? I can stop by. I forgot to leave those donations with you yesterday anyway."

"Eight in the morning, if that's not too early. You can have breakfast with us. It's the least I can do." Jenna didn't give him a chance to say another word. She sprinted down the sidewalk with Sadie in her arms. He was worried for her, for how tired and stressed she looked. She'd always been so strong and passionate, but her eyes looked dull and defeated. She'd mentioned a divorce. A rebellious thought of hope anchored in his mind, but he cast it away as far as it would go. The woman had left him to go off to a university and never returned, never wrote, never called, and certainly never came home. Not until now, but now was too late.

CHAPTER FIVE

Saturday morning, Jenna busied herself cleaning the house of cobwebs and dust. She spent all day unpacking boxes and putting things away, except what required storage. Those supplies would have to wait for the furniture the county had ordered for the school to be delivered Monday.

Sadie helped put her clothes in her drawers like a good girl, and they made her bed together. She'd done well considering all the change. Actually, Sadie had done better since they'd left Shane than she ever had.

Sadie dropped her pillow to the floor. "Oh, oh, oh." She danced around then eyed the door to the bathroom.

Jenna held her breath. Was she really going to go in the potty? She watched her daughter scurry across the floor and into the bathroom. Moments ticked by and Sadie hummed, but she didn't hear anything. Then the magical sound of tinkling filled the room. Jenna danced around with the pillow, holding in her squeals of delight. She'd done it, and on her own.

The toilet flushed and water ran for a few seconds before Sadie came out with her shirt half tucked into her pants. "Mama, Mama, Mama. Did it!"

"You did, honey!" She lifted Sadie and twirled around the room.

"Weeeeeee!" Sadie flung her head back and enjoyed the ride.

Jenna knew the doctors were wrong. Her little girl was able to do whatever she wanted to in life; it just took her a little longer to get things right. "I'm so proud of you."

She reached for the phone, ready to call Shane to tell him the news, only to realize he wouldn't care. It was so big, but she had no one to share it with. It was news she'd share with her husband, father, or mother. But one was gone, another dead, and the other wanted her gone. It didn't matter, she had Sadie.

Her phone buzzed in her hand, and she looked down at the display. She hesitated only a second before answering. "Hey, Mama. Guess what?"

"What?" Cathy said with her thick southern drawl.

"Sadie went in the potty all by herself."

There was a pause on the other end, and Jenna knew her mother didn't realize the gravity of what had just occurred.

"Tell her that Devon and I are proud of her. Actually, why don't we go out and celebrate."

Jenna paused. What was her mother up to? She seldom did anything without an ulterior motive. "Celebrate?"

"Yes, and well, I don't think our conversation went so well last night. Darling, I love you and I'm excited you're home, but I have something I need to tell you.

Can you meet us at the diner? I want an excuse to see my granddaughter again anyway. I feel like I barely know her, and I hope you'll let me be the best grandmother I can to her since you'll be living in town."

Jenna glanced at Sadie. She felt like going out and celebrating. This was the biggest, happiest thing in their lives in a long time. "Sure, we can meet you. How about in a half an hour? Sadie will be getting hungry by then."

"That sounds great. See you at six at the diner."

The phone clicked off and Jenna tossed the last pillow on the bed. "We're gonna go out and celebrate. How does dinner at the diner sound? We'll see your grandmother and grandfather there, too." Jenna wasn't sure how to refer to Devon. It felt like a betrayal to call Devon her grandfather, but Jenna's father had been gone a long time, and Sadie never knew him. Jenna had loved her father deeply and always dreamed of him knowing her children, but that wasn't to be.

"Yes, yes, yes." Sadie ran upstairs and opened her drawer. "Boo."

Jenna reached her bedroom and saw her hold out her favorite blue sweater. "That's fine, baby, but you have to promise to stay with Mommy, okay? You can't leave my side, got it?"

"Aha, aha, aha." Sadie slipped the sweater over her head, covering the long-sleeve purple shirt she already wore. Good thing the sweater had a high enough neckline to hide the purple, or she'd look like an Easter egg that had soaked in dye a little too long.

Jenna unbuttoned her favorite flannel shirt, the one

she'd lived in for years, and put on a fresh T-shirt, sweater, and pants before she slipped her feet into her brown boots. All the while, she kept Sadie in sight. She'd only taken a three-minute shower while Sadie slept today. If she didn't figure out how to keep Sadie safe, she'd have to take up camp showering soon.

They headed downstairs. "If you want to walk, you'll need to wear your jacket and we'll have to leave now to give us extra time."

"No jacket." Sadie crossed her arms and stuck out her bottom lip. "Noisy."

Jenna picked up the jacket that had been the battle between them for three weeks now. She understood Sadie didn't like the noise the material made when it rubbed together, but she needed to stay warm in this chilly fall weather.

"Sorry. No jacket, no walk."

Sadie tapped her foot and stared her down. She could be so stubborn when she wanted to be, but Jenna needed to be Mom and Dad for her now. If she coddled her too much, she'd never grow up.

"'Kay." She slid her arms into the jacket with a cringe and snarl.

Jenna went to the coat rack then turned to find Sadie at the front door with her arms outstretched like a scarecrow, so they wouldn't touch. She giggled. This was going to be a fun walk to the diner.

The evening sun dipped beyond the trees and she thought better of walking, but this was Sweetwater County. There wouldn't be an issue walking at night.

They made their way to town and up to the diner,

Sadie tiptoe walking the entire way. It didn't matter though, she'd gone potty. One thing at a time. That was how it would work for her. Today praise for the potty, tomorrow working on walking.

Jenna entered the diner with a new sense of hope. Not just for Sadie and their new life in Creekside. Not just for being closer to her mother and getting to know her stepfather. A little hint of hope for Drew flickered in the back of her mind. He hadn't been wearing a ring, and she felt the chemistry between them when he pulled her into him. Could she ever forgive him for cheating on her? For getting another girl pregnant when he swore to always be faithful to her? Perhaps.

"Hi, Jenna. Over here." Her mother waved, but the expression on her face looked like a possessed pumpkin.

The diner hadn't changed much over the years. It had the same fifties-style décor with red vinyl topped bar stools, booths, and tables. Jenna made her way across the checkered floor, around a waitress and two tables, to reach her mother and Devon. "Hi there."

"Look at you. I think I know what Sadie's favorite color is." Devon bleeped her nose.

"Booo!"

"That's what I thought. You look awful pretty this evening. Would you do me the honor of being my date? I thought we could go sit up at the bar and order our food and get to know each other while your mother and grandmother talk."

Jenna moved one-step closer to Sadie. "I'm not sure that's a good idea. She tends to get lost often. You've got to keep your eyes on her constantly."

"Don't worry. You can sit facing them, and Devon won't let go of her hand except for her to eat. Okay?"

Jenna reluctantly released Sadie's hand. "You stay with your grandfather, okay?"

"Grandfather? I like the sound of that." Devon smiled, a big granddaddy kind of smile.

Jenna couldn't help but smile back. "I hope that's okay."

"Absolutely. I'd be honored. Okay, little one. Let's go see what kind of trouble I can get us into."

They headed for the front bar area and Cathy scooted onto the far bench, leaving the other open so Jenna could keep an eye on Sadie.

"I wanted to apologize." Her mother twiddled her fingers and took a long breath. "I never meant to make you feel like you're not wanted here. That's the farthest thing from the truth. You just surprised me, that's all."

"Then why'd you tell me to leave? Are you upset about the divorce that much?"

Her mother shrugged and placed her palms flat against the table. "No, but what happened? Why'd you two break up? I thought you were happy?"

"We were, until Sadie arrived. After that, things changed."

Cathy scooted closer. "I get it. Kids can complicate things, but—"

"He didn't want Sadie, Mama. I had a choice. Commit her to an institution or leave."

Her mother gasped, cupping her hands over her lips. Her eyebrows were higher than when she discovered

Jenna kissing Drew behind the bleachers at a football game. She dropped her hands to the table with a loud slap. "You can't be serious. He actually told you that?"

"Word for word. And if you think I'd ever choose a man over—"

"No, never. You did the right thing. I can't believe Shane doesn't have the sense God gave a billy goat. I thought he was a good man, could provide well for you."

"I know, Mama. You always wanted me to marry well, but that didn't bring me happiness."

Her mother sighed. "But Drew would have," she mumbled.

"Maybe, but that doesn't matter now. What happened in the past will stay in the past. It's time to move forward." Jenna lifted her chin and waved to the server.

"Jenna, you need to know something." Her mother twisted her fingers into a pretzel. "It's about Drew and what happened in high school."

The bell over the front door jingled and the diner filled with laughter. Jenna looked up and saw Jessica, her arm hooked in the crook of Drew's. She stood on tiptoes and kissed him on the cheek. A girl, around nine years old, pranced around them.

Jenna felt the room spin. She thought she could handle this, prepared for it, but seeing it in person was much different than facing the reality hundreds of miles away.

She couldn't breathe. Her lungs contracted with such intensity she thought she'd pass out. There had to be a way out of there, a way that didn't involve facing Jessica and Drew, but the front door was the only way out. Without another word, she darted to Sadie and took her by the hand.

"No, no, no, Mama. Eating. Fun," Sadie protested.

"No time, we'll eat ice cream at home." She grabbed Sadie a little more aggressively than she meant to, making Sadie yelp. "Sorry, baby."

"No, no, no," Sadie protested again, kicking, shoving and pinching. She hated change. Transitioning in any form was difficult for her, but Jenna had no choice. One more minute in there with them would destroy her.

"Jenna, wait. I need to tell you something," her mother called after her, but she headed for the door with Sadie in tow.

"Jenna?" Drew called. "Jenna, wait."

She scooped Sadie into her arms and ran. Ran so no one would see her cry, or collapse, or fall apart.

CHAPTER SIX

Drew slid his hand from Jessica and grasped the front door, but Cathy stepped in front of him.

"We need to talk." Her pressed lips and determined brow, yet sorrow filled gaze told him to heed her warning.

"What have you done, Cathy? I've known you a long time, long enough to know this isn't going to be good news."

Jessica took a step away from him toward Trianna. "I'll go save us a table."

This wasn't fair to her. The girl had been nothing but kind to him over the years, but he knew Jimmy was right. He'd never be available to another woman until he had answers about why Jenna had left. He turned back to Cathy. "Why is it you always seem to be at the heart of trouble?"

Devon clutched Cathy's shoulders. "Please, Drew. Can we speak outside, or better yet, at our home?"

Drew analyzed Devon West. The man was honest and had worked magic with Cathy. If nothing else, he believed in this man. And it was time he started facing the fact that he'd been lying to himself all these years.

He'd never moved on from Jenna, and it was time to have answers so he could let the past go. "Give me a minute."

Devon nodded, wrapped his arm around Cathy's shoulder and led her out the door. The air around him felt heavy with foreboding. Perhaps he should stay in the diner with Jimmy, Trianna and Jessica. Stay away from the promise of answers that never came. No, he didn't just owe it to himself, he owed it to all the other women who never measured up to Jenna.

With a knot in his gut, he sat next to Jessica and faced Jimmy and Trianna. Jessica stroked Tally's hair and whispered for her daughter to be patient.

"Listen, guys. I owe you an apology. Jessica, I am truly sorry for the drama."

Jessica placed a delicate hand on his. "I understand. No need to apologize. I know Jenna returning after all this time is difficult for you, and I think you should go and speak to her."

Why couldn't he be in love with this beautiful woman, with her bright blue eyes, soft lips and curves in all the right places? She was kindhearted and had always been a friend. Perhaps once he faced what happened with Jenna, his heart would be free to find something new.

"Tally, you going to hang with your mom tonight for me?"

Tally rolled her eyes and sighed. "I guess, but I'd rather be at my sleepover."

"Go. I'm a big girl. Besides, I have a lot to do. We'll be moving to Riverbend next week for a job." She gave a bright smile, one that said everything would be okay.

"You're amazing," he said.

"Yes, she is." Trianna reached out to her friend, and Drew knew he'd get an earful from Jimmy on Monday.

He kissed Jessica on the cheek and waved bye to Tally. "I hope this new job is a good thing for you both. I'm sorry you'll be leaving, but you'll be less than an hour away. Tally, I'll be going to the father-daughter dance with you next month." He slipped away, his heart stuck between making things right for Jessica, and knowing he couldn't without answers. It was time. It was long past time.

Cold air whistled through the alleyway beside the diner. He paused, still torn between returning to Jessica and giving her the attention she deserved, or diving back into the world of Jenna. There was no choice, not if he ever hoped to move on with his life.

With a determined step, he walked the couple of blocks to Cathy's house. The home Jenna grew up in. He stood out front, eyeing her childhood bedroom window. The one he'd climbed the trellis to only a few days before she disappeared. The same trellis he'd planned to climb to ask her to marry him.

He swallowed the memories with a bitter taste, marched through the iron gate and up the front steps.

Devon opened the door and gestured to Cathy sitting at the kitchen table, her face paler than snow. "I think you should have a seat." Devon said.

Inside, the décor had changed slightly, but most of it remained as he remembered. He crossed the living room to the kitchen and lowered to a kitchen chair across from Cathy.

Devon stood behind her with his hands on her shoulders. "Go ahead. You need to tell him and Jenna the truth."

Cathy trembled and Drew's instinct told him to comfort her, but he remained with his hands clasped in front of him. "What do you need to tell me?"

"I-I don't know where to begin," Cathy said, her voice cracking.

"How about starting with what happened ten years ago when Jenna disappeared? When you told me she deserved better and that I should let her live her life without me."

Cathy's entire body shook and tears streamed down her face. "I was wrong. I was so wrong. I can't believe the man I told her to marry turned his back on his own daughter."

Devon rubbed her shoulders. "You can do this. Go ahead."

Cathy took a stuttered breath. He wanted to shake the answers out of her but forced himself to wait for her to gain composure.

She straightened and lifted her head, blotting the running mascara from under her eyes with a crumbled tissue. "I was a different person back then. I wanted what was best for my daughter, but I was wrong. I was so wrong. Now, I realize that losing my daughter forever is a sacrifice I have to make if I want her to find happiness. And I think you are the only person who has ever made her happy since her daddy died. You see,

Jenna didn't leave you the way I told you she had. She wanted to stay here, to marry you, raise your children, and live happily-ever-after in Creekside, but I wanted more for her. She wasn't recovering from her father's death. The only time she got out of bed was to be with you. I couldn't watch my bright, vibrant daughter wilt away. I had to do something."

"If she didn't want to leave, why did she? It doesn't make sense. There was nothing that would have made me leave her."

"You're right."

Drew rubbed his palms down his face. "You're not making any sense."

"She left because you got Jessica pregnant."

Her words sucker-punched him, shoving his breath from his lungs and causing his gut to spasm. "What? No, that never happened. It wasn't me."

"I know."

Drew shoved his chair back and paced the floor, unable to remain still any longer. "Why would Jenna think that? Why wouldn't she talk to me? She believed you and left me?"

"No. It wasn't just me. After I told her she went to confront you, but when she found you Jessica was in your arms."

"Wait. What? We never—"

"She saw you under the oak tree, holding Jessica. The tree she always said she'd marry you under some day."

His memories flipped through like an old-fashioned rolodex until it fluttered to a stop at the image. “Wait, I was comforting her. She’d found out she was pregnant and the father claimed it wasn’t his. We were friends, that’s all. Jenna knew that.”

“She knew what I told her, and then found you with Jessica under that tree. Even after that, she didn’t want to believe it, but when she confronted Jessica, she admitted she was pregnant.”

“Jessica told her that?”

“Not that you were the father, just that she was pregnant. She didn’t even know what Jenna thought was going on. I exploited it and told her she had to let you go. That the baby deserved a father and that she needed to leave Creekside. She’d just lost her own father, she’d never keep a child from having one.” Cathy took a deep breath and blew her nose into the tissue. “I had applied for University of Tennessee on her behalf. I handed her the acceptance letter and sent her to school. She didn’t tell anyone where she was going because she thought you’d find her. She sacrificed herself for the chance that you’d find happiness and be a good father to your child. Now, she’s back.” Cathy clasped her neck as if the confession stung on its way out.

“And she saw me with Jessica and her daughter tonight.”

“Yes.” Cathy shuttered. “I sent her away from a good man. One who's willing to go out with a woman who has a daughter that isn’t his own, for a man who wanted his own daughter put in an institution because she's unique. I was wrong. I was so wrong.” Cathy broke down and Devon took her into his arms.

"By coming clean, Cathy believes that Jenna will never speak to her again. I don't believe that, but she's willing to sacrifice her relationship with her daughter so that you might make Jenna happy. I hope you do." Devon gave him the man-stare. One that a father would give to a boy picking his daughter up for a first date, but this wasn't a first date. This was a hot mess of lies, deception, and life-altering manipulation.

Anger filled him. Anger he hadn't felt since he was a teenager. He needed to leave this home, needed to get away from Cathy and find Jenna. He headed for the door without a word.

"Son, I suggest you take a few minutes to process all this before you go find Jenna. You need to decide what you want. Jenna was just as much of a victim in all this as you are. Remember, she was willing to give you a chance to be a good father. Make sure you allow her to be a good mother."

Devon's words followed him out the door. Anger, grief, and emotions that didn't even have names pummeled him. Not knowing what to do or where to go, he walked. Walked through town, walked through the park, walked through all his memories, and still found no answers. He sunk to the damp ground underneath the large oak tree and raked his fingers over their initials. Brittle bark fell from the promise of forever.

CHAPTER SEVEN

Jenna woke to a monstrous been-crying-all-night headache. How could it hurt so badly after so long? Why did she feel so betrayed? Drew had a right to be with whomever he wanted. Heck, they had a child together. She'd just read too much into their connection. It was familiar and she was on the rebound from a horrible divorce.

"Mama?" Sadie crawled into bed and snuggled into her side. The smell of her apple shampoo and the softness of her fine curls relaxed Jenna.

"Potty. Happy?" Sadie drew small circles on Jenna's hands.

"Oh, honey. I'm so sorry. You never had your treat, did you?"

"Potty, Mama. Again. Happy?" Sadie pinched her hand out of frustration. Something they'd been working on since the divorce.

"Sadie, we don't pinch, remember?"

She bowed her head and pinched herself. "I sorry."

"Are you telling me you went potty again?" Hope washed over the rough terrain of her heart, and seeped through a few cracks.

"Yes, Mama. Yes!"

Jenna hugged her tight. "Good girl. I'm so proud of you."

"Big girl. Happy?"

In that moment, Jenna realized something. Her little girl was trying to make everything better, but that wasn't her job. "I'm very happy. I tell you what. Instead of going out for ice cream today, let's go to the store and buy all the toppings you like, and then we'll come back here and have a picnic.

Sadie clapped three times. "Good, Mama."

Jenna sat up and held Sadie in her lap. "You are doing so well, Sadie. You are talking more and going potty. I think this was a good move for us. How do you feel?"

"Happy, Mama." She clasped Jenna's face and gave her a sloppy kiss on her cheek. "Mama happy?"

In Sadie's world everything was black or white; there was no grey area. How could she explain she was sad, but happy with Sadie's new accomplishments? It was best to put on a brave front and make this right. She'd be the best mother she could be to her little girl. Perhaps even her mother could help on occasion. She wanted Sadie to have lots of people to love her, and Devon would be a big part of that since he was the only male role model in Sadie's life now. He was a good man, had to be a saint to put up with her mother. Heck, a magician for changing her so much. Still, that little twinge of resentment for replacing her father remained.

She would return the dozen messages her mother left last night after she made some coffee. No need to add to her headache before fully caffeinated.

Three knocks at the front door catapulted Sadie off the bed. She ran down the stairs in her little blue nightgown and straight to the front door.

"Sadie, don't open the door."

The door squeaked open before Jenna reached the bottom of the stairs.

"Hello. Is your mommy here?" Drew's voice penetrated the walls of her home, threatening the safety of her heart.

"No. Mama sad. You bad." Sadie crossed her arms over her chest and stomped her foot. "Go."

Jenna froze at the bottom of the stairs, searching for words to say, but they all jumbled together in her sorrow.

He knelt down. "I'm sorry. I didn't know, but I'm here to explain."

Sadie reached out, grabbed a hunk of skin on his arm, and pinched. Jenna jumped into action. "Sadie, we don't pinch people, no matter how bad they are."

"I sorry." Sadie folded her arms over her chest and bowed her head.

"It's okay. I understand that you're angry, Sadie. You're a good girl to protect your mother like that. I'm afraid I need to speak to her, though."

"There's nothing to say. I overreacted. You and Jessica have a right to be together. You're obviously good with children and—"

"Her daughter isn't mine," Drew blurted.

She heaved a quick breath and that was when she noticed how disheveled and out of sorts he appeared.

"What are you talking about? She's around nine, right? That's when you two..." She couldn't form the words, they choked her speech until she could only close her mouth.

"I didn't know you thought that, but it isn't true. None of it's true. Listen, we need to talk. I don't think we should in front of Sadie, though. Can we step outside?"

Jenna shook her head. "No, I'm afraid not. The fence is broken and I can't take my eyes off her. She'll disappear on me."

"Right." He slid his fingers through his unkempt hair. He looked like he hadn't slept all night.

"Sadie, would you like to watch a show?" Jenna didn't know why, but she wanted to know what Drew had to say. She should slam the door in his face and never speak to him again, but that got her nowhere last time.

"Yes. Yes. Yes." Sadie toe-walked to the room next to the kitchen, took out the laptop and started her video.

"I think I need coffee." Jenna waved him inside and shut the door. "I could call my mother and see if she could watch Sadie for a bit while we talk if you'd like."

"You haven't spoken to her since last night, have you?"

She shook her head then grabbed the glass coffee pot and turned on the faucet. "No, she's left me a dozen messages, but I didn't feel up to it."

"I'm sorry. I know I didn't do this, and part of me

is mad at you for believing, but another part doesn't want you to suffer."

She poured the water into the maker and slid the glass carafe into its place. "What are you talking about? You're not making sense."

"Jenna, maybe I should let your mother tell you, but to me she's lost that right and I can't wait a second longer. I've been walking all night. I slept under our tree." His voice cracked and his eyes misted.

She lowered to the chair by his side. "What is it?"

He closed his eyes and took a long breath. "I hate to tell you, but I want to all at once. It'll hurt you."

"Tell me." Jenna sat straight up.

"I never knew why you left, and I couldn't find you. Your mother told me it was because you didn't want to be trapped here with me for the rest of your life. I couldn't believe that, so I tried to find you but no one would help. I even waited four years in case you returned after college."

"You didn't marry Jessica?"

"No, Jessica and I have only ever been friends." He dropped his fists to the table. She'd never seen him so emotional and distraught. "Her daughter isn't mine. I never slept with her."

"But my mother said—"

"She lied to keep you away from me. I'll let you work out the details with her. I can't explain the why."

"But Jessica said she was pregnant when I confronted her and then I saw you under our tree with her."

Drew shook his head. "I was comforting her

because my dirt bag of a friend told her it wasn't his, that he was going away to college and would never think of her again."

Jenna's head spun. She shot up from the chair, but dizziness took hold. She grasped the table and stumbled toward the coffee pot.

"Say something."

Jenna grasped the handle and squeezed until she thought it would break. "All this time. All the pain." A million memories mixed in her brain, and she'd never be able to decipher them all. "You thought I left you?"

"Yes," he said, his voice deep and hollow.

"And I thought you'd cheated on me."

"Yes."

Jenna lifted the coffee pot to pour, but her hands shook too much. Her body shook, her life shook.

He was there in an instant, holding her steady, the way he had when they were kids, the way he could have always been holding her, but she'd left. She left without even asking him the truth.

"I did this. I left."

He guided her hand to place the pot back in the machine. "I won't lie. I thought that, too, but I think I understand your reasons. I spent all night thinking back through everything. We were kids, naïve and uncertain. It was your mother, and we both know how persuasive she can be."

"My mother. She did this to me. All these years. I tried to follow the right path after leaving here. I thought my mother knew better than I did after I...I thought you'd slept with Jessica. I married a man she approved of and thought would be a good husband. I might have even loved him at one point. I don't know. I don't know anything anymore." She turned to face him, and the lost years in his gaze. Anger bubbled to the surface. "I can't believe she's kept this from me all these years. Lied to me, deceived me. What kind of mother does that?"

CHAPTER EIGHT

Drew couldn't hold himself back any longer. Despite the niggling of resentment for her believing he would cheat on her, he had to touch Jenna.

She leaned her head to his chest. "I'm so sorry. I'm so, so sorry."

He wrapped his arms around her and held her tight. "Shh, it's okay."

The only sound in the small home was music from the laptop where Sadie sat mesmerized by the screen and the theme music to some kids show.

After a few minutes, Jenna looked up. With puffy eyes, she shook her head. "You must hate me."

He brushed her hair from her forehead and sank into the depths of her forest green eyes. Eyes that always made his heart soften and his thoughts calm. "I won't lie to you; there's been enough lying. I hold some resentment that you'd believe something like that about me, but in my mind I know why. I understand, but it'll take a while for my heart to catch up with my brain."

She cleared her throat and pulled away. "I can't ask for more than that. I'm sure you've moved on with your life and that you just needed some closure. You have that now. We both do. I need to focus on Sadie. Since the divorce it's just been the two of us."

Drew didn't like where the conversation was leading. He didn't know what he wanted, or what he expected, but he couldn't just let her go. "Don't."

She rubbed her forehead until a red spot remained. "Don't what?"

"Don't shut me out."

Jenna poured coffee then leaned against the counter with her head down. "You'll never truly forgive me, and you don't even know me. I'm a different person now." She faced him and lowered her voice to a whisper. "I'm divorced and I have a child with special needs. I'm about to start a new job. I have no time for anything else in my life. It's not fair to you, even if you're not already involved."

"I'm not."

Jenna handed him a mug and placed hers on the table. "Not what?"

"Involved." He sank to the seat. "Jenna, I never moved on from us. There was never another. I mean..." He half-chuckled at the conduct of his youth. "...I've been with women."

Jenna's lip twitched the way it did when she didn't like something. Could it really bother her that he'd dated others? Did she still care?

Jenna traced the rim of her coffee mug. "I don't need the details."

He took one of her hands in his. The warmth of her flesh sent a zing of heat through him. "You're right, we don't know each other. We are different people than we used to be. Perhaps we won't like each other, but we need to talk. We need to see who we are and what, if anything, is still between us."

"Sadie—"

"Is a beautiful, sweet young girl, and I'd love to get to know her. I'm not her father. From what your mother said, I'm nothing like him."

"That's a good thing," she blurted, but then squeezed the cup tight in her hands. "I can't believe she did this. I'm so angry. It's taking all I have not to go straight over to my mother's house and disown her for the rest of my days."

He chuckled. "I'm kind of surprised you're taking it so well. I remember a day when you'd tell your mother what for. Heck, you're handling it a lot better than I did last night."

She glanced toward her daughter, and he saw all the love he once possessed in her eyes. "I'm a mother. It's no longer about my needs. Sadie already woke upset because of my state last night. I need to be better for her. I need to be stronger. Honestly, I can't see or speak to my mother right now. Maybe some day, but not now. I'm not sure what happened to me, but somewhere in the last decade I lost myself. I said I returned to Creekside for the job, and that is completely true, but it's more than that. The last time I felt whole was when I lived here. I thought maybe I could find myself, find happiness again if I came home."

Drew covered her hand with his. "I can't make any

promises, except two. I won't lie to you. And I'll be here for you and Sadie in whatever way we decide. Even if things aren't meant to be between us, I'll still be here."

"Funny." She blew out a sharp breath.

"What's funny?"

Sadie laughed nearby and they both glanced over before Jenna leaned closer to him. He caught a whiff of floral shampoo, a new scent from what he remembered. "Her biological father, the man I married, abandoned Sadie. Now a man, a man who I hurt, is willing to be here for us. I guess part of me can't believe you won't change your mind. That you won't decide we're too much for you."

He cupped her cheek, sliding his thumb up and down to feel her soft skin. "I've had all night to think about this, and I want to get to know the new Jenna, the one that's here now. You just found out, so I won't ask you now, but when you decide if you want to get to know the slightly overworked, underpaid, confirmed bachelor cop of Creekside, then let me know." He stood, but he couldn't bear the thought of walking out that door. It took several long seconds for him to reach the hallway before he heard the chair scoot from the table behind him.

"Yes."

He gripped the corner of the wall, stopping himself before he could move another step. "Yes?"

"Yes, I want to get to know the current Deputy Sheriff Walker."

He spun on his heels and closed the space between them, his arms ready to hold her close, but she held up a hand. “Slowly, for Sadie’s sake.”

He awkwardly patted her shoulders. “Understood.”

She giggled, a sound that filled the room and made him smile. It was the same kind of laugh, but a little less free. “I tell you what, I promised Sadie that I’d go to the store and get some ice cream. I’d promised her one last night, and the night before but she never got it so we’re going to make ice cream sundaes and have a picnic on the floor.”

“Sounds perfect, but what if we take Sadie to the park?. There is a new ice cream place near there and we can eat it outside. There won’t be many more beautiful days left to enjoy outside. Sadie can swing—”

“Swing?” Sadie jumped to her feet and clapped. “Aha, aha, aha.”

“I think you have the Sadie seal of approval.” Jenna looked down at her robe. “Well, I guess I should get Sadie and I dressed.”

“If you have to.” He sighed.

“I can see some things haven’t changed.” She winked, an adorable, playful, sexy wink that made him swallow hard. “I guess most of the unpacking’s done. I’ll receive the new computers and supplies tomorrow, so I’m free for awhile. Sadie, let’s go get dressed so we can go to the park.”

She didn’t have to repeat the words before the little girl raced upstairs, her nightgown fluttering behind her.

“We’ll only be a few minutes. Why don’t you enjoy a cup of coffee? If you don’t mind, can you grab a travel mug out of the cupboard next to the coffee maker?”

"Sure." He rounded the corner and found the cups in the cabinet. Jenna and Sadie probably hadn't even had breakfast yet. Heck, he hadn't eaten since yesterday afternoon. Combing through her refrigerator, he found some eggs, bacon, fruit and milk. He searched the bottom cabinets and found an electric skillet from the early 1980s. He set it up on the counter and unplugged the coffee maker, toaster, and a phone charger from the wall.

After a couple of minutes of frying some eggs and bacon, Sadie danced into the room. Her little hips twisted and turned to make the tutu around her waist move. "Pink."

"Yes, it's pretty pink."

"Bacon!" Sadie squealed and crawled onto one of the kitchen chairs.

"And eggs."

"No eggs. Yellow."

He plated an egg and several strips of bacon and set it on the table. Sadie crossed her arms and stuck out her bottom lip. "Yellow."

Jenna entered the kitchen, wearing jeans and a green and burgundy sweater that fit in all the right ways. "Wow, you made breakfast? You have changed."

He laughed. "Yep, no burning toast. Do you remember when I set off the fire alarm at your house?"

"Remember? The fire department showed up when Mama saw the smoke and called them. That's when she threw you out, saying you weren't in the house at a respectable hour."

They both laughed. It felt good to remember,

instead of trying to forget.

"Mama, yellow," Sadie groaned and pointed one finger at her plate.

Jenna sighed. "It is so sweet of you to make us breakfast, but I'm afraid we have some food issues that we're working on. Sadie won't eat anything yellow right now."

Drew noticed Jenna twisting her fingers and realized she was worried how this would affect him. "How about orange? Is orange okay?"

"Aha, aha, aha."

"Then how about some orange slices and bacon?"

"Aha, aha, aha."

Drew retrieved the plate, slid the eggs onto his own plate, and sliced a few oranges. "Hey, I unplugged a few things. You need to be careful having outlets overloaded since the wiring is old in this house."

The doorbell rang and they both froze in place.

Sadie leapt from the chair and darted to the front door.

Jenna raced after her, but it was too late. Sadie swung the door open to Cathy standing on the front porch. And based on her expression when he caught up with Jenna, her mother wasn't happy to see him.

CHAPTER NINE

Jenna ground her teeth and fisted her hands but kept her mouth closed. One, two, three steps until she reached the door and managed to breathe.

"Gamma." Sadie waved.

"Sadie, go finish your breakfast." Jenna didn't break eye contact with her mother, but listened for Sadie to skip back to the kitchen.

Drew remained at her side. "Do you want me to go?"

Jenna laced her fingers through his and squeezed tight. "No, the only person leaving here is Mama."

Her mother lifted her chin. She looked determined with her set jaw but defeated at the same time, the way her swollen, red eyes drooped. "I see you couldn't wait to tell her."

"Don't you dare blame anything on him. This is you. This is all you, and right now I don't want to see you." Emotions threatened to take hold, but she fought to maintain control. She wouldn't give her mother the pleasure of seeing her upset, not to mention she didn't want Sadie to see.

Drew squeezed her hand back and she was thankful for the connection. "Yes, I told her everything, so there's no need to say it again. I think Jenna's been through enough."

"I'm her mama. I need to explain."

Jenna gathered all the strength she had left, which wasn't much, and squared her shoulders. "You need to leave and you need to not return unless invited. And trust me, that won't happen anytime soon. Now leave, Mama."

"Jenna," her mother pleaded, which only added fuel to her simmering emotions.

"No. This isn't about you, Mama. Sadie's here, and I'm not willing to upset her right now. She's been through enough. For once, think of someone else before yourself. Now leave."

Her mother's chin trembled and the lines around her eyes deepened. "I'll leave, for now, but sometime soon we'll talk. You can't avoid me forever. Not if you're planning on staying in Creekside, and based on the way you two are holding hands, you'll be staying."

A gust of wind brought leaves down onto the front lawn and Sadie ran out the door to chase them. Cathy stepped between her and the street.

"Play me?" Sadie scooped up leaves and threw them in the air, giggling.

Cathy placed a hand to her chest and glanced at Jenna. She stood firm, chin held high, but Jenna wasn't going to let her ruin the day.

"I'm sorry," Cathy said, squatting down to meet Sadie at eye level. "I have to go for now, but I'd love to play with you another time."

Sadie stopped for a moment and glanced between all

of them, her head tilted to one side. In that moment, Jenna was positive Sadie caught on to more than people thought she did. "I play." She dove into the pile of leaves and rolled around.

Cathy traipsed across the lawn to her car and backed out of the driveway. Once she reached Main and drove out of sight, Jenna let out a long breath.

"You okay?" Drew tucked her into his side.

"No, but I have to be. Listen, I wouldn't blame you if you wanted to do something else today. I'm afraid I'm not the best company and I know this is a lot to take on right now. There'll be plenty of time for us to see each other."

He placed one finger over her lips. "Shh. Not gonna happen. Let's get the dishes done and take Sadie to the park."

Sadie chased a golden leaf fluttering through the air.

"I'm gonna have to ask questions about Sadie," Drew said, "so don't take them personally. I just want to make sure I'm doing things right with her. Can I pick her up, or does she mind physical contact?"

"She loves contact. Actually, she craves it. Except the back of her neck, that's a no touching zone."

His lips curved into a relieved smile. "Good. I'll get Sadie and clean up. You go finish anything else you need to, and we'll take her to the park." He bolted off the front steps before she could protest and swept Sadie up into a spinning tornado of leaves. How did a man who had no children relate to her child better than her own father, a man who never touched her unless necessary? It was as if Sadie'd had the plague for the last four years and now she'd been cured.

Drew and Sadie entered the house with bits of leaves in their hair. Jenna managed to pull them from Sadie's hair and set her up at the coffee table with a small puzzle to keep her busy. Drew shook his head over the trash can, but he still had specks of leaves caught in his hair. She stood on her toes and slid a few fragments free.

She wobbled and he held her waist to keep her steady then bowed lower so she could reach. The closeness made her pulse quicken, and her finger dexterity seemed to vanish. After four tries, she gave up on the last few bits.

"Get it all?" Drew asked.

"Most of it." Jenna lowered her heels back to the floor and to her disappointment, Drew released her and turned to the dishes.

"What's this?" Drew tugged a sticky note from the dishwasher she hadn't even noticed yet. "I guess the dishwasher needs some work. Looks like Maverick will be over next weekend to make a few repairs to the house. He's been busy at the new VA Center." He handed her a dishtowel and turned on the water. "I'll wash if you dry."

The man had changed, for the better if that was possible. He was domesticated. Of course, with the way his mother had always been out of it from drinking, Drew had to learn domestic skills. He washed and rinsed a plate then handed it to her. Their fingers touched and they both remained a second longer than needed. The second and third dish, fourth—each time they touched a little longer than the last.

She enjoyed the normalcy of dish washing but never knew it could make her heart beat faster. After the final dish, she reluctantly handed him the dishtowel and retrieved Sadie from her world of puzzles. "Time to go."

Drew grabbed his keys from his pocket. "I can drive. We'll just need to transfer Sadie's car seat."

Jenna decided not to argue. If he drove them then he'd have to drive them home, which gave them more time together.

They drove down Main Street toward the other end of town. Memories of making out, drinking and all sorts of other high school shenanigans came flooding into her mind. She chuckled as they passed the set of swings.

"What's so funny?" Drew asked.

Jenna shrugged. "I was remembering the time that we all went to the park at midnight when I was supposed to be spending the night with Marsha. We had to run from the police, or my mother would've grounded me for life. Now, you *are* the police."

He laughed, a hearty, full of life sound. "Yeah, I doubt anyone in Creekside would've guessed I'd be enforcing the law when I was a teenager."

"Ice cream," Sadie reminded them.

Drew guided his crew cab pickup truck into a space at the edge of the park. "Yes, hon. It's just a little walk from here."

She clapped and unhooked the belt over her car seat.

"Whoa there." He reached around and tickled her tummy. "We don't want you to get hurt by a car from a car. Let your mama get to the door first."

Jenna hopped out and opened Sadie's door, but she didn't bolt into the middle of the street. Instead, she lifted her sweater to show her belly and said, "Again, again, again."

"I thought you wanted ice cream."

She gasped and covered her mouth with a tiny hand then lowered her shirt. "Aha, aha, aha."

"Then we'll pick up this tickle fight later." He rounded the car and placed his hand on the small of Jenna's back, ruffling her inner feathers in a good way. "I've got her."

He slid between Jenna and the car and lifted Sadie into the air before tossing her up and catching her. He was strong. Jenna hadn't been able to toss Sadie into the air for two years despite her thin frame.

Sadie did a jack-in-the-box smile and dance with her arms. His biceps strained the seam of his shirt. He had grown into a handsome man, strong, rugged, yet gentle.

He caught her gaze transfixed on his arm and grinned. "You coming, or are you just going to enjoy the show?"

Heat flushed her cheeks and she turned, pretending to spot the ice cream shop.

Sadie clapped. "Ice cream." She pointed down the street at the sign with a picture of an ice cream cone.

Jenna spotted Judy Benjamin headed down the street toward Main with a woman by her side. She waved and the two women stopped to wait for them to cross the road.

"Hi, darling," Judy said. "This is Mrs. Ruth Turner.

She's the secretary to Commissioner Rogers."

"Hello. It's nice to meet you."

The woman held out her hand. "It's a pleasure to meet you in person. I was excited when you accepted the position. How's the building working out for you?"

"It's great. Sadie and I are settling in all our personal items upstairs, and we're ready for the delivery of the computers and supplies tomorrow. I have so many great learning games for the children."

Mrs. Turner frowned. "I'm sorry, but there won't be a delivery tomorrow. I'd planned on telling you in the morning when you came by the office."

"Oh." Jenna hid her disappointment. She wanted everything set and ready to go before the opening of the school in two weeks. "I understand, delays happen. When should I expect the delivery?"

"Well, you'll receive bed mats, dishes, and other various supplies you'll need on Tuesday."

Jenna nodded. "And the computers?"

Mrs. Turner pressed her lips together as if frustrated at Jenna's lack of understanding. "There'll be no computers. The board didn't approve the budget for that portion of the program this year."

Sadie squirmed in Drew's arms and he lowered her to the ground, but Jenna took hold of her hand immediately. "I don't understand. How will I teach the students if I don't have any computers?"

"We're not expecting miracles, honey, just a place for the children to go at the end of their normal school day. And for those who are not in school yet so the parents can work."

A triple shot of anger, disappointment, and disbelief injected into Jenna's system. "Are you saying the center is going to be a glorified daycare?"

Mrs. Turner waved her hand and waggled dismissive eyebrows. "No, more of a respite care for families. It's a program that will provide a much-needed service to the residents of Creekside."

Jenna shook her head and fought with Sadie to keep hold of her hand, her patience dropping quicker than the fall leaves around them. "I have a degree in special education. Why would you advertise for a teacher if you only needed a para-pro, or someone to take care of babysitting?"

"We couldn't hire any babysitter. We needed someone that understood the unique needs of the children who cannot attend regular daycare. I know your mother is against this, but don't let her influence you too much."

"My mother?" Jenna cringed at the thought of Cathy West being involved in this, or in her life.

"Yes, she came by early this morning and tried to convince Mr. Rogers that they didn't need the center and then said you weren't right for the job. I guess she thinks you deserve better, but I must reiterate that you'll be helping a lot of families in this town if you remain."

Jenna fisted her hands, wanting to tell the woman that her mama had nothing to do with this and that she had no right to try to have her fired. She had only wanted Jenna gone so she wouldn't find out about Drew and her lies.

Judy cleared her throat. "It sounds as if there's some discussions that need to happen between Ms. Greyson and the county. I'd hate for us to waste an opportunity with such a well-trained professional that can offer more than just babysitting services. Why don't we speak to the board at the next meeting? I'm sure Ms. Greyson can convince them of the additional needs."

Jenna wanted to tell them that the county misrepresented themselves and that they needed to fulfill their promise, but one glance at Judy told her to hold her tongue.

"I guess that couldn't hurt," Mrs. Turner said. "I'll put Ms. Greyson on the agenda for the next board meeting." The woman turned one pointed high heel shoe toward Main, but paused. "Ms. Greyson, I hope you realize how important you are to this town. We truly need you here. Even if the board doesn't approve the funding, it's still a step in the right direction. Judy, make sure she realizes her worth. After all, you're the one who convinced the board to hire her." She sauntered off with the rapid click of her heels on the sidewalk.

Sadie got loose and ran toward the shop.

"I'll get her, you finish talking. We'll meet you inside when you're done." Drew trotted after Sadie and caught her a few steps from the door. "You know, munchkin, you keep running off like that and I'm gonna have to hog-tie you."

She peddled her feet in the air and twisted, but he kept hold of her.

Once they'd disappeared inside, Jenna turned her

focus back to Judy. "Why did you fight for me to get this job? Did you know what my mother had done? About Drew?"

Judy nodded. "I'm aware of the lie she told you ten years ago."

"Then why bring me back here? Why have me uproot Sadie and my life only to show up here for a job that's something any high school graduate could do. Don't get me wrong, I am not above hard work, but that's why I want to do more. I went to school to study teaching so I could help children with unique learning needs. I want to provide a proper education for those kids."

"I understand, but sometimes things take a while to come around in a small town. You may not want to hear this, but you could sell a Bible to an atheist. You inherited your mother's gift of convincing people of what they need to do. I know you can talk that board into what's right. No matter how you look at it, there's a need here that only you can fulfill."

Jenna didn't want to listen, but Judy had a point. Either that, or Judy was better at manipulating people than her mother. "I'll talk to the board, but you need to tell me why you got this job for me. I feel like you had an ulterior motive. You and my mother were tight. I know she told you what she'd done. If you knew, why'd you get me to come here? I mean, I hate her. It's her fault I lost all those years when I could have been with Drew. I love my daughter, and I don't regret or wish anything to change that would alter that, but I left because of a lie."

Judy popped her hip out and placed a hand on it. "Did you?"

"Yes. I loved Drew. I've always loved him."

"Then why'd you leave?"

Jenna huffed. "Stop playing games. You know why."

"Yes, but do you? Why didn't you speak to Drew before you left Creekside?" Judy asked.

Jenna fought the memory of seeing him with Jessica under the tree. "I didn't have to. I saw him with Jessica. My mother told me what he'd done."

"Since when did you ever listen to your mother? You two haven't seen eye-to-eye since you were old enough to talk back to her. The Jenna I knew would go to the ends of the Earth to prove her mother wrong, especially about her boyfriend. But that time you didn't, you left instead. You didn't even leave a forwarding address with your friends from high school."

Jenna shifted between feet. The conversation all the sudden stifled her with warning. "I don't know what you mean. I left because I thought Drew cheated on me."

"You sure about that? Before you put all the blame on your mother, think back and be honest with yourself. Don't misunderstand me, your mother was completely wrong. I'm just saying you need to make sure you face why you truly left Creekside."

Jenna opened her mouth to protest, but the words didn't come. She shook her head and tried again, but still the words escaped her. The image of her leaving in the night, her bags packed and not stopping to see anyone, did seem strange, but she'd done that so she wouldn't have to face the embarrassment of telling people that they'd broken up and why. She shook her head again, but with each whip of her hair, an ounce of truth seeped into her consciousness.

CHAPTER TEN

Sadie threw her head back each time Drew pushed the swing in the quaint Creekside park. The little girl was so full of life, she was intoxicating. On the other hand, Jenna had become withdrawn, silently rocking on the swing next to Sadie. He tried not to think too much about it. She'd been through a lot in one day.

"So, they won't provide the necessary tools for you to do your job? Yep, sounds like county politics. I wouldn't take it personal. You know, the county administrator is the one who fought for this. You should talk to him at the board meeting and tell him how critical it is. I'm sure with a little persuasion he'll come around."

"You really believe that?" Jenna asked.

"Yes, I do. If not, I'll give him a parking ticket every time he double parks outside his office until he changes his mind." Drew pushed Sadie again and she leaned back enjoying the ride, her pink tutu fluttered in the wind.

"You'd do that for me?"

"I'd do a lot for you, Jenna. You deserve the best."

She sighed. "I don't know about that."

The sadness in her voice made him long to cheer her up and let her enjoy life the way she used to. "Don't let this thing with the money and job description get you down. You'll figure something out. If you're still the Jenna I once knew, you'll have them begging you to take the money. You can't give up yet."

Jenna straightened, her back rigid, her chin tipped high. "I won't," she said with determination. She looked dazed, as if capturing a memory, and mumbled, "Not this time."

He tried to read her thoughts, but her lost expression only confused him more. Perhaps she was regretting leaving her husband, giving up on the marriage. From what he understood, she had no choice. What kind of parent would institutionalize Sadie?

Some children chased each other around the merry-go-round, and by the way Sadie sat straight and eyed them, he guessed she wanted to join their fun. "You'll get the money, trust me."

"You're right, I will. I took an undergraduate class that discussed grant writing. If I'm going to do the things I hope to, I'll need more than just county funds anyway. I'm going to need a way to transport the kids, to utilize the latest technology, and have a sensory gym."

"A sensory gym?"

She chuckled. "Yes, sorry. I'm getting obsessed about this again. It's been a dream of mine to provide the right kind of methodologies each individual child could need. The schools do the best they can, but I didn't want to work under the constraints of the public school system. I wanted to offer something more, a place for them to move and learn at the same time. To learn their strengths and encourage them. I've kind of combined the philosophy of my undergrad degree in therapeutic recreation and my masters in special education. A sensory gym is a place where children who seek stimuli, like Sadie, will feel secure and receive what their body needs while learning."

He loved the fire in her eyes. The way her passion excited him made him want to help. "See? You've already won me over. I have no doubt you'll win over the commissioners, too."

She sighed. "I hope so. I'd like to try to make this work. If not, there isn't a place for me here."

Drew's chest ached at the thought of her leaving again, to the point he couldn't even think about it. He wanted the subject changed and quick. He wanted to make her see that he was worth staying in town for.

"Do you remember when we came here after the homecoming game our junior year?" Jenna asked.

An inner light glowed with the memory. "Yes. How could I forget? We were swinging right here next to each other. Jimmy and his girl had gone off on a walk and you looked at me and told me you loved me."

"Yeah, and you fell off the swing." She brushed her light hair from her eyes and dug her shoes into the sand beneath her. "I thought you were going to run away and never return."

No doubt deciding she wanted to join the other

children on the teeter-totter, Sadie leapt from the swing and landed like a perfect gymnast. For a second anyway, before she fell back on her pink tutu. Before he could see if she was okay, she climbed to her feet and raced off to the teeter-totter.

He took a seat on her empty swing and nudged into Jenna. "You kidding? I fell off the swing because I couldn't believe how lucky I was. I'd fallen in love with you the day Mr. Brown made us partners on that project, and you told me to get over myself and do my own work."

"Ha, that's right. You were used to the girls doing whatever you told them to."

He shrugged. "What can I say? It was a gift."

"From what I've heard, you kept that gift. Word has it you've been the playboy of Creekside."

Was that what was bothering her? She was worried he was playing games with her?

He twisted the swing to face her and took both her hands in his. "Jenna, I only dated superficially. I never committed to a girl since you."

"Why?" Jenna's eyes misted.

"Because." He glanced at Sadie then back at Jenna. "I never got over you. You were the one that got away."

Jenna analyzed the sand on her shoes. "I see. So I was the only girl that you never had."

"No, Jenna. You're the only girl I've ever loved. You may have been the first one to say it, but I felt it for far longer."

Jenna's shoulders lifted then fell twice before she squeezed his hands. "You should have gone on with your life. I'm so sorry that you were left with so many unanswered questions."

"I could hold onto the anger at your mother, or the disappointment I felt when I discovered you believed I cheated on you, but life's too short and you're here now."

Jenna took a stuttered breath. "I don't want to hurt you again. Not like that."

"Be honest and you won't. I know you're scared, I can see it in your eyes." Drew stood and tugged Jenna from the swing. "I know you've been through a lot with your ex-husband. I'm sure your trust in others is shattered after he turned his back on you and Sadie, and then you discovered your mother's deception. But don't shut me out. I'm not asking for a happily-ever-after here. I'm asking for right now, a moment to take a breath and get to know each other again. I promise to give you time to figure things out. I know Sadie is the most important person in your life, and she should be." He tipped her chin so she'd face him. "Trust me."

"I don't know if I can."

The teeter-totter thumped every few seconds and the sound of Sadie's giggles confirmed her proximity to them. He nudged closer. The floral shampoo soothed his anxiety and he tucked her hair behind her ear so he could steal another look at her gorgeous green eyes. "You know, I think you're still the prettiest girl in Sweetwater County. The prettiest girl I've ever seen."

She snickered. "Does that usually work on girls? Smooth, Walker."

"I don't say that to all the girls, just to the ones that

have haunted my dreams, day and night, for over a decade."

Her arms trembled and he tucked her into his side to keep her warm, walking her over to the bench near the teeter-totters.

Jimmy rode by in his cruiser and waved. He returned the gesture but didn't make his way over to speak to him. He'd get an earful soon enough about his behavior toward Jessica and how Jimmy had been right to call him out about Jenna.

"You two have remained friends all these years?"

The cruiser headed toward Main and took a left toward Jimmy's home. Thankful he didn't stop, Drew settled back on the bench and Jenna joined him. "Yep, we didn't see each other much when he was married to his first wife. She really did a number on him. I thought he'd never take a chance on someone again, but Trianna changed all that."

"She must be pretty special."

Sadie tumbled off the back of the teeter-totter and Drew shot up to scoop her off the ground, but Jenna snagged his hand. "She's okay. She'll just cry if she thinks she should."

The softness of her skin hadn't changed. And her eyes, her eyes nearly did him in. He cupped her cheek and she lifted her head. Her lips, full and calling to him, parted. In that moment, he wanted to kiss her, to reconnect with her, to hold her in his arms and never let her go.

He didn't care who might see them in the park. Let everyone in Creekside see, the county, no, the world. If he could steal one kiss, he knew she'd remember how they were together and never want to leave.

He lowered back to her side and cupped her face. She leaned into him and his pulse raced faster than the kids playing chase.

Only inches from tasting bliss, she turned her head and looked away. An awkward silence remained between them. There was no way to play off the fact he'd just tried to kiss her and she rejected him.

"I'm sorry. I just..."

"No need to explain. Taking things slow, remember?" He stood and offered his hand. "I'm afraid I have to get you two home. I have a shift this afternoon, and I have a few errands to run before that."

Jenna took his hand and stepped into his personal space, their bodies nearly pressed together. "I do want to kiss you. I just want to make sure that there's something here besides memories. Deep down I know that if we move forward too quickly, and it doesn't work out, then we'll never have another chance. And I have Sadie to think about." She stood on her tiptoes and pressed her lips to his cheek.

It felt like a kiss goodbye.

CHAPTER ELEVEN

Jenna looked over her wish list for the center then scanned her project proposal for the board of commissioners. After another sip of coffee, she took a breath and felt a new sense of pride for the work she'd accomplished. It might have taken most of the night, but at least she felt more prepared to meet with the board today.

She stretched then began digging through some pictures on her laptop for examples of some of the strategies she'd used with Sadie. Visual aids always helped sell a point. She clicked through years of photographs and pulled a few into her presentation document for the board. Jenna had been in the trenches so long fighting for Sadie that she hadn't realized how much she'd accomplished despite the odds.

Jenna found the folder with Sadie's baby pictures. She had spent a month digitizing those old photos. She was a beautiful baby with her bright eyes and wisps of strawberry blonde hair.

A folder labeled *High School* caught her attention and she clicked on it. Senior prom and graduation photos popped up on her screen. She glanced through them, her pulse quickening at the sight of Drew and her. They looked like children back then. Not that they were old now. Drew still had that strong jaw line, but his body had filled out more in all the right places. She sighed and leaned back, eyeing their happy times memorialized in a big photo collage she had made her senior year.

Could she be that happy again? Why did she ever leave? Judy had a point. If she'd truly wanted to stay, why didn't she go confront Drew? Perhaps she didn't want to stay. Maybe the thought of remaining in Creekside frightened her, like it frightened her now.

Two raps at the front door made her stiffen. She'd had her phone off all night since her mother wouldn't stop calling. Did that woman really have the nerve to show up here this early? With one more stolen glance, she captured the sight of Drew's smiling face and kept it close while she went to face her mother.

With a determined step and a ready-to-fight attitude, she swung open the front door. "Mama, I told you—"

Drew stood there, holding a computer screen in his hands. He shook his head. "Not your mama. And I hope you're happier to see me." His gaze dipped down and she realized she was standing there in an open robe and her nightgown that barely grazed her mid-thigh. The corners of his mouth nearly stretched to his eyes, his hungry eyes. "I should've called, but if I keep showing up unannounced, I get to see you without your clothes on."

She closed her robe and tied it around her waist, a deep heat spreading from her chest up her neck all the way to the top of her head. “Um, yeah, don’t go saying that in public or people will talk.”

He hovered close to her face. “Okay, I’ll just say I’ve seen you in the morning with a towel wrapped around you and in a skimpy nightgown. That sounds better, right?”

She slugged him in the arm. “Stop.”

“Well, I won’t have to if you leave me standing here any longer. Someone will eventually pass by and see you in that with me at your door.” He winked.

She snagged his sleeve and pulled him inside before glancing up and down the street to make sure the gossips of Creekside hadn’t caught sight of them. Deciding it was a clean escape, she shut the door and turned to him. “What are you doing here? And why do you have that?”

“Geesh. Good morning to you, too.”

Jenna rubbed her eyes and stifled a yawn. “Sorry, that came out wrong. I’ve been up all night working. I don’t think there's enough coffee in the world to wake me up right now.”

He set down the screen and shuffled toward her. “I could help wake you up.”

Her body quivered at his words. “Excuse me?”

“Where did your mind go?" he asked with a smirk. "I see you haven’t changed. I meant we could go for a run, or get some exercise. That always works for me.”

“You must be tired a lot.”

“What?”

Jenna bit her bottom lip. “Nothing. I need to get some more work done.”

“Well, that’s why I’m here. This isn’t a social call. It's all business.” He straightened his shirt and put his hands on his hips. “I’m here to drop off some blankets, pencils, pens, and other supplies the town put together before you even arrived. I’ve got a few extra things I picked up last night from the school board, a local preschool, and the veteran’s center that I’ll set up for you.. Also, Julia will be here in about an hour to help you with the grants. She’s written a ton for the veterans facility. Her husband, Maverick, is going to take a look at adding some outlets when he comes to fix the dishwasher. He’s the one that donated this house and did all the renovations.”

Jenna tried to wrap her mind around everything he just said.

He closed the distance between them and touched her chin with his knuckle until she closed her mouth. “You’re not used to having people help you, are you?”

She couldn’t breathe, couldn’t move with him so close to her. She wanted to lean into him in one breath and run away the next. She finally managed to shake her head.

“Well, welcome home. You must’ve forgotten that our town is a family and we help each other. You convinced me that this center is extremely important.”

“I don’t know what to say. You’re amazing.”

“Well, I can’t act like I don’t have any other motives for helping than the children. A part of me knows you’re not going to remain in Creekside if this center doesn't open, so I'm no saint."

"Still, I can't accept all this help. It's my job."

Drew placed a hand at her neck, sending goose bumps down her arms. "Let me help you. Let *us* help you. This job is bigger than one person, and I know this is important to you."

Every inch of her settled into the comfort that was Drew, allowing the words to flow freely without the interruption of fear. "Thank you."

He paused and eyed her, the same look he had the night before when he went to kiss her. She wanted to let him know it was okay this time. It was the right moment to see if what they'd had still existed between them. Sadie was asleep upstairs, and they were alone. She took a half step toward him and took a long breath. Anticipation pricked her skin.

They hovered next to each other for a moment, making her truly want to feel his lips touch hers. She lifted onto her toes and he met her halfway, but instead of kissing her, he tilted his head and whispered in her ear. "You're not ready, and I'm not going to push you."

He backed away and turned to the front room where he left the computer screen. His fingers ran through his hair and laced behind his head. Back muscles rippled with his movement, stretching his shirt tight across his shoulders.

Something about him turning his back to her made her want to kiss him even more, but instead of attacking, she retreated to the safety of the kitchen to pour them both some coffee. She pressed her palms to the cool countertop and took a moment to collect herself. The excitement awakened her more than the caffeine, filling her with renewed energy.

"I'll take a cup if you have extra before I unload the truck."

"Unload it?" Jenna handed him a warm mug full of black coffee. "No cream or sugar, right?"

"You remembered?"

"Of course. We used to take a thermos with us when we went hiking early in the morning. I learned to enjoy mine the same way by the end of our first month dating."

"I asked you if you wanted me to put cream and sugar in it."

"I know, but we were just getting to know each other and I didn't want you to think I was some sort of wimp."

He lowered his cup to chest level and chuckled. "There are many words I could use to describe you, Jenna, but wimp is not one of them. You're one of the strongest and bravest women I've ever known."

Jenna refilled her cup and leaned against the wall in the hallway. "Yeah, right."

He sat at the kitchen table and leaned back, resting his left foot on his right knee. The man pose, the one that most men relaxed into when they were trying to look cool. "I only know a little about what happened with your husband, but from what I do know, you stood up to him. You were brave enough to leave and face an uncertain future so that your daughter would get what she needed in life. You returned home to a place you left a decade ago, to work a new job that allows you to spend more time with your daughter. You discovered your mother lied to you, yet you haven't gone off on the crazy train out of town. I'm in awe over how well you're still holding it together. Most people would've cried themselves to sleep last night over the news that the job they'd been looking forward to wasn't what they thought. They'd give up and leave. No, from the looks of what's on this table, you were up all night fighting. You're a fighter, Jenna. I think you've just forgotten that, forgotten who you really are."

She wished she could see things the way Drew did. He'd always been the most amazing person she'd ever known. Giving, optimistic, and handsome beyond what should be allowed.

"Go get dressed. Maverick and Julia will be here soon. I'll bring in the tables and the chairs we borrowed from the elementary school, and the two computers that were donated."

"Computers? Really?" She wanted to jump up and down and clap like Sadie, but she kept her composure and instead squeezed his hand, the only way she could think to show her gratitude. At the moment.

"Go ahead and get ready. I'll bring the stuff in and you can show me where you want it set up."

Jenna spun on her heel and jogged to the stairs. "Give me a second and I can help you carry it inside." She raced upstairs and checked on Sadie, who was still sound asleep. Score! She could take a quick shower and not worry about her escaping. With renewed energy, she hopped in the shower, washed her hair, dressed in her favorite faded plaid button-up shirt and jeans. If only she had time to dry her hair and fix it. She hadn't done that in a long time. Oh well. She tied it back, snagged her cell phone from the nightstand, and raced downstairs where she spotted Sadie helping Drew bring small plastic chairs in from his truck.

"Mama, I help," Sadie said, her tone high with joy.

"She's the best helper ever," Drew shouted over his shoulder, his back to the house. The truck wobbled as he walked across the bed then jumped to the ground. He dusted off his jeans and grabbed a wooden table that looked like it was newly constructed and the perfect size for two kids. Three steps toward her, he glanced up at her, dropped the desk and stood with his eyes wide, scanning her from head to toe.

She looked down, self-conscious of her frumpy appearance. "I didn't have time to do much with myself." She tugged nervously at the hem of her shirt. Shane had hated it, insisting she throw it out, but it had always brought her a sense of comfort, of home. "If you don't mind giving me a minute, I'll go change and dry my hair."

He walked around the desk and ran a hand down the sleeve of her shirt. "You still have it."

She blinked at him, feeling like she'd just walked into the middle of the conversation. "What?"

Sadie stumbled on the stairs next to them, but recovered quickly.

"The shirt. It's from our first camping trip," Drew said, his voice deep with emotion.

No, it couldn't be. She hadn't kept it all these years. But how long had she had it? She'd worn it often over the years, because it was the most comfortable shirt she owned, and it always smelled good. She'd had it ever since...high school. She touched the soft fabric and remembered the camping trips in the mountains with all their friends. "Yes, I still have it. It's my favorite shirt."

A truck pulled up behind Drew's and a woman hopped out of the driver seat. A little boy joined her. She waved and a man rolled around the car in a wheelchair. "Hey, man. How's it going?"

Drew about-faced and greeted the man, giving him a hearty handshake. "Good to see you. Thanks for all your help last night getting these tables made."

Drew had worked all night making furniture? And his friend had helped?

"This is Jenna. She's the one I told you two about. Jenna, this is Maverick, Julia, and this little man is Ryan."

Jenna offered her hand to the two adults. "It's nice to meet you. I can't thank you enough for helping with this."

The young boy grabbed two chairs and headed to the steps where he handed them to Sadie. Julia placed her hand to her chest. "I totally get how this works. I've been in charge of the veterans' center, and I was lucky enough to have Trianna Mason's help with grant writing. So I thought I could pass on the knowledge. Not to mention a 101 course on how to deal with county politics."

Jenna's phone buzzed and she glanced down, figuring it was going to be her mother again, but to her surprise, the display showed *Sweetwater County Government*. "I'm sorry. Please excuse me for a moment." She answered the call with her breath tight in her lungs. "Hello?"

"Hello, is this Ms. Jenna Greyson?"

Jenna switched ears, as if it would help her recognize the voice on the other end better. "Yes, it is."

"I wanted to call to let you know that the county board meeting has been moved up."

Jenna's breath hitched. "What do you mean? It's going to be tough to have anything ready before next week. How many days do I have?"

"You have nine hours. The meeting is this evening."

CHAPTER TWELVE

They stood in the parking lot outside the county offices, and Jenna fidgeted with her dress, holding tight to her stack of documents. Drew wanted to reach over and pull her into his arms and tell her she could do this, but with the parking lot full of commissioners heading into the building, he feared the display of public affection would do more harm than good. She needed to appear strong and ready for a fight.

Sadie ran in circles around them until she grew tired and leaned against the side of the truck.

"I'll wait with Sadie while you go into the meeting," he offered.

Jenna's eyes flashed fear and he knew she wanted him by her side, but they couldn't leave Sadie alone.

He spotted Judy, James, Cathy, and Devon walking up to the front door, so he turned to Jenna. "Be right back." He trotted to the front of the building before Jenna could stop him. "Judy, I have a huge favor to ask. Would you be able to watch Sadie while Jenna speaks in the meeting? She wants me in there with her but I don't think Sadie should be in there distracting her. She won't be able to concentrate if she's worried about

Sadie running out the side door all the time."

"I can watch my granddaughter," Cathy said, her chin in the air.

Drew had to fight the urge to tell her she didn't deserve time with her family. "I think it would be best if Judy watched her for a bit."

Sadie skipped over and took Devon by the hand. "Nose?"

Devon squatted. "Oh, I can probably return that to you now. If you'll give mine back, too."

She giggled and pushed her hand against his nose. Devon tweaked hers then stood. "I can hang with Sadie. I'd like to get to know my granddaughter better anyway. We can go to Café Bliss and have some hot chocolate. James, would you mind dropping Cathy at the café after the meeting?"

"Not a problem," James said.

Drew looked between them until Judy smiled and placed a hand on his. "It's okay. Devon is a good man and capable of watching her. And Cathy will stay with us."

Jenna and Julia walked up. "Remember, you need to convince them that you have a great idea and they're getting a deal with your proposal," Julia said.

"Got it." Jenna nodded.

"We're here to support you, dear."

Jenna shot a sideways glance at her mother. "I thought you didn't want me to have this job."

Cathy bowed her head with obvious shame. "I was being selfish, trying to keep you from the truth, but I'm here now."

Judy cleared her throat. “Jenna, Devon’s going to take Sadie for hot chocolate. He’s great with kids and I know he’ll be great with her. I thought Cathy should remain with us.”

Jenna’s eyes bounced between them all and settled on Sadie who clung to Devon’s leg.

“Sadie, do you want to go with Devon to get hot chocolate while Mommy’s in the meeting?”

Sadie bounced. “Aha, aha, aha.”

Jenna sighed. “Okay, but Devon, please make sure she stays in your sight at all times. Our little Sadie tends to disappear quickly.”

“I promise not to take my eyes off of her for a second.”

"Okay. Thank you." Jenna took Drew’s hand, sending a jolt of warmth through him. “I guess we should get inside.”

They all funneled into the lobby and found their way into the large meeting room. The chairs set up for the audience was already full of people. Several women wore red hats and Cathy West pulled one from her oversized bag and joined the women. Jenna watched her, but he nudged her toward the front of the room. “Let’s take our seats.”

The commissioners already sat at the front of the room, occupying tables situated in a crescent shape. Jenna halted and squeezed the papers tight to her chest. He could feel the tension in her hand. “You’ll do great. Trust me.” He kissed her cheek and took a seat, silently praying she would win over the board and stay in Creekside.

"This meeting is now called to order," a woman seated at the commissioner's tables said. "If you would refer to your agenda, you'll see that our first order of business is in regards to the children's Center for Autism. Jenna Greyson will be speaking. Ms. Greyson, please approach the podium."

Jenna walked to the front, her face whiter than the papers in her hands. If he could speak for her, he would. This entire charade was the cost of small town business, but he knew she could win them over with her passion and expertise.

She cleared her throat and shifted through the papers, shuffling and reshuffling.

"If you are not prepared, Ms. Greyson, we can reschedule you for next month," Commissioner Rogers said.

Jenna's entire body stiffened and her chin lifted. That was the woman he remembered, the fighter, the winner, the passionate woman.

"I'm ready, sir. I'd like to thank the commissioners and residents of Creekside for allowing me this opportunity to speak about my plans for the center. I've only just arrived, but I'm already aware of the desperate need for the center."

"We are all in agreement that the center is a necessity to Creekside, Ms. Greyson. Our question is how to properly utilize funding for this community services program."

"Yes, I'm glad you are in agreement. This *is* a service, not a respite care facility."

The commissioner leaned forward into the

microphone to argue his point, but Jenna barreled on.

"I currently hold an undergraduate degree in therapeutic recreation and a master's degree in special education. I've studied various modalities and completed my thesis on therapy through active movement. During my study and internships, I realized that both my undergrad and graduate work were a winning combination for increasing learning for children with unique needs. That being said, there is not one mold that will fit every child. What I hope to offer is an individualized program for each child in Creekside that requires a different modality for learning new skills."

"Do you have any evidence that your theory will work?" Commissioner Rogers asked, his tone softening slightly to a pessimistic level of interest, instead of closed off to everything she had to say.

"I'm glad you asked. Yes, I have statistical information that backs my theory of active learning." Jenna rounded the podium and placed a packet of information she'd created on the top of the center table.

"Yes, well, we all know about statistics and how they can be molded to fit the practitioner's intentions," Commissioner Rogers said.

Cathy stood, and it took all Drew had not to shove her back into her seat. "If I may, do you have any experience with this theory? Have you personally put it into practice and found favorable results?" Her question sounded rehearsed, well thought out. Just what game was she playing with her daughter?

"Yes, I do." Jenna returned to the podium and held

up a picture of Sadie on a large ball with a full smile on her face, showing it first to the audience then to the board. "When my daughter was only two years old, we were told she'd never be able to learn her numbers or the alphabet, read, ride a bike, or even be potty trained. She was diagnosed on the autism spectrum. Specifically, she was diagnosed as PDD-NOS—Pervasive Developmental Delay, Not Otherwise Specified—and it was determined she was grossly behind for her age. We tried the common therapies and found some success. The behavior therapies helped with her eye contact and eating, but she wasn't progressing in the other areas. One day, while bouncing her on a ball I began to sing the numbers. On the third round, she joined in and sang the first five. In two minutes, she learned more than she had in two years of her young life. That's what fueled me to pursue my thesis."

"And has your daughter developed any further, or has she plateaued?"

Jenna's shoulders rose and she dug through her papers until she brandished a picture of Sadie on a small trampoline. "This is how she learned to count to fifty and to sing her alphabet."

Rogers's eyes widened and he leaned forward. "Any other further progress, say on potty training?"

"Yes, I'm happy to say that now my daughter is learning to communicate. Other areas of her life are developing as well. She is now saying one- to three-word sentences and her frustration is decreasing. She is happy and playful with little more than mild outbursts of pinching."

"Do you believe that you can achieve the same success with other children?"

"Yes, sir."

Commissioner Davis pulled her microphone closer. "This sounds like an ambitious project. I know many of our residents, including board members, have struggled with their children's progress. What makes you believe you can do more than our public school system can?"

"I'm not saying I want to replace current systems. I'm offering an opportunity to work with the school system and provide after school care, therapeutic outings, parent training, and structured play that will bring about learning. The reason this will assist in the learning process is because it'll be tailored to the individual child, not a group of children with the same diagnosis."

The room remained quiet for a moment. Drew held his breath, afraid the board would shut her down as they had during other meetings he'd attended. Davis eyed Rogers. "This sounds expensive. Not only the equipment involved but to do outings? The parents would need to take off of work to drive their children."

"No, ma'am. I'll only need one parent volunteer, unless I receive additional funding for an assistant at some point. And I'll have a van for transportation."

Commissioner Davis chuckled. "Van? Assistant? It sounds like you're requesting a major increase in funds that the county does not have to offer."

"No, ma'am." Jenna retrieved some papers and

handed a copy to each of the commissioners. “As you can see, I’ve outlined here what the operating expenses will be for the center. I’ve already applied for a grant that’ll provide a fifteen-person passenger van. Another grant will provide ten thousand dollars for construction changes to adhere to ADA requirements, which our current facility isn’t completely compliant with. This will allow us to build an addition onto the center for a therapeutic gym, with a ball pit, ropes, and other equipment.”

“I see here you’re applying for over a dozen grants. What are your chances of receiving any of them?” Rogers asked.

“Extremely high." Several murmurs erupted from the audience, but Jenna plowed on. "There are also four others that will allow funds for computers and adaptive technology, and I’m also working with Riverbend University to start offering an internship program for students. This will allow us to have some free help while sharing my knowledge with the university students.”

“I do see an additional request for funds, though,” Commissioner Davis said.

“Yes, ma’am. Those are for operating costs to fuel the van and to repair equipment, and the rest are outlined on the itemized list at the bottom. The reason for these items are that some grants will only be awarded to facilities that show they are able to operate the entire year without financial difficulties. By showing the county backs the program, it opens the door to not only receiving these grants, but for additional funds."

Drew couldn't help but be proud of Jenna. She was a passionate and eloquent star at that podium.

"Wow, it sounds like the county has a win-win here," Cathy nearly shouted.

Jenna didn't respond. She remained with her eyes on the board. *Good girl.*

"This operating budget still exceeds what we've approved," Davis said.

Mr. Burton stood. "Yes, but Ms. Greyson has shown that this can bring additional funding to the county, which may lead to more employment. The neighboring towns don't have a center for special needs children so it's highly likely families from outside our town will bring their children to learn here. While other small towns are being deserted due to the unemployment rate, we need to consider these opportunities. This can lead to contracting jobs, additional support staff, and more."

Commissioner Davis laced her fingers together as if she was about to pray. "Everyone in the room knows why you want to see this center succeed. If you make sure there are funds, your daughter, Rose, will return home to work with the center in the summer. If there's no center, Rose will not return to Creekside."

Drew wasn't a fan of Mr. Burton, but he found Ms. Davis's directness underhanded. Of course, most of the town knew she never wanted the center in the first place.

Commissioner Davis leaned back and glanced down the line of board members. "I suggest that we table our decision until we can verify the information presented to the board today. We'll have a meeting next month to share our findings and call this to vote."

"A month?" Jenna asked, an air of desperation in her voice.

"Is there a problem with that?" Commissioner Davis asked.

Jenna straightened her jacket. "Yes, ma'am. Some of these grants are time sensitive."

"That may be, but we won't be rushed into a decision without properly verifying this information. Perhaps we should consider re-evaluating this next year and proceed with our initial plans for the upcoming fiscal year."

Jenna shook her head, her strawberry blonde hair waving like fire. "With all due respect, ma'am, early intervention is critical. According to my information, there are eight children in this county under the age of seven that would benefit from the center. In a single year, statistics show that their rate of learning new verbal, motor, and socialization skills will decrease and they will become even further behind their peers."

"When do you need a decision in order to submit those grant proposals?" Commissioner Rogers asked.

"By the end of the month."

"Well, that doesn't give us much time," Commissioner Davis said. "The Thanksgiving Feast is next week, which is one of the oldest traditions of our town. We cannot call a meeting during that time."

"No, but we can call a special meeting the Monday after Thanksgiving. Will that work for you, Ms.

Greyson?" Rogers said.

"Yes, the timeline will be tight, but I'll have all proposals ready for submission." Jenna sounded calm, in control, but Drew knew her better. She was screaming and jumping for joy on the inside.

The county commissioner raised his gavel. "Then we will revisit this at a special meeting on Monday, the twenty-eighth of November at seven o'clock. And Ms. Greyson, I will be checking your data on the success of this play therapy." His gavel struck the table and Jenna gathered her papers, turned, and marched from the room.

Hope flooded Drew like a raging river. He rushed out after her and took her into his arms. "You were amazing. That's the Jenna I know. That fire and determination when you know you're right is breathtaking."

She flung her arms around him and held him tight. "I can't believe they're even considering it, especially with how little time I had to prepare. I thought I was a goner there when Ms. Davis challenged me."

He leaned back and looked down at her, the passion in her eyes had returned. He'd found the old Jenna. "No, she just added that little nudge needed to hit your fight button."

"My fight button?" Jenna cocked an eyebrow at him.

"Yes, the one that gets you riled up and no one can stop you."

She laughed, a sound of relief and happiness. "I guess I do have a fight button. It just hasn't been pushed in a long time."

“You did great, dear,” Cathy said.

Jenna stiffened in his arms. “I didn’t need your help.”

Cathy toed the carpet in the lobby with her black boots. “I know you didn’t. I guess I just wanted to show you how much I want you to stay in Creekside. But honestly, it was more than that. What you said in there sounds exactly like what Creekside needs. Despite our differences, I love my home and the people around me. I only want what’s best for them.”

“Yes, well, we all know what your kind of love can do,” Jenna said, but he felt her body wince at her own words.

“I see." Cathy's face fell but she recovered quickly. "Well, I’ll be heading out with Judy and James. I hope someday you’ll be ready to talk to me, but I realize after what I did it’ll take a long time, if ever. I guess I’ll just have to keep trying.”

“If you keep coming around, all you’ll do is make me want to leave Creekside. I won’t live the rest of my life with you interfering all the time.”

Drew held tight to Jenna, her words burned him to the core with fear. He couldn’t let Cathy drive her from Creekside again, but how could he stop her?

CHAPTER THIRTEEN

Jenna felt exhilarated for the first time in years. Something inside her had snapped when she was in front of the board. She'd gotten her point across and the board was willing to discuss the issue further. There was no guarantee they would approve the funds she needed, but she didn't feel beat down. She felt alive, working toward something she believed in for the future of her town.

My town? It had been years since she'd thought of Creekside as her town. When was the last time she even participated in an event? It was probably the Thanksgiving Feast the year that she moved away. Yes, that was the year her father died. They had a place of honor set at the table for him, as they always did when the town lost another citizen.

She eyed the old Hatfield Inn through her side mirror. She remembered Old Lady Hatfield at the Thanksgiving Feast that year. The woman made a huge speech about her ancestors and the great feud. Jenna's mother had told her the woman wasn't crazy, she'd just spiked her own pumpkin punch. The kids all ran around the table, chasing a dog and creating quite the ruckus.

Had Sadie ever been to a function where everyone was laughing and sharing and playing? No, she hadn't. Did she want to go? It would be so good for Sadie to spend some time with kids her own age, but Jenna would have to face her mother and deal with her meddling shenanigans. Perhaps if she went with someone, like Drew. That would give her a mama buffer, and she couldn't think of anyone else she'd rather go with. Heck, the thought of him leaving for work and her not being able to see him until tomorrow made her sad. It was like when they were younger, and every time he left she couldn't wait for him to return.

"Drew?"

He turned on his signal and pulled into a parking spot across the street from Café Bliss. "Yes?"

"Would you like to go to the Thanksgiving Feast with Sadie and me?" She held her breath, not sure if he'd say *yes*. Was she crossing a line?

He shifted into *park*, turned off the truck and faced her, an epic Drew smile spread wide across his face. The kind that usually made women know they were in trouble.

"I've always volunteered to work the event, so I'm not sure I can take off."

Great, she'd just made an idiot out of herself by asking him out. She grasped the door handle to escape. "Sure, I understand."

He snagged her arm. "No, you don't. I'd love to go with you to the Thanksgiving Feast. Would you mind if

I was in uniform while we're there?"

She fought the urge to throw her arms around him again, even though it felt so right earlier. Instead, she shrugged, trying to be cool about it. "I don't mind. Sadie would probably like that. She likes uniforms."

"I hope her mother does, too. Some women say I'm sexy in uniform."

Jenna tried to steady her breath. "I see the rumors are true about your way with women."

"Now, Jenna, you grew up here. You know better than to listen to small town gossip." He playfully chucked her chin and opened his door.

She continued to work on steadying her breath and composing herself before he opened her door and helped her from the truck. But that last assault had her nerves jumping all over again. She could manage to get out on her own, but his hands on her hips felt too right to protest.

He shut the door and looked around them before he whispered, "Besides, I couldn't think of another woman I'd rather be tied to."

She gulped so loud the entire county probably heard it.

"In the three-legged race. What were you thinking? Geesh, Jenna, I thought we were going to take things slow." He laughed and tucked her into his side. Yep, he knew the affect he already had on her. She needed to get control of herself before this got out of hand too quickly. She needed to maintain distance until they really knew what they had between them. Heck, she wasn't even sure if she was staying in this town. If the board voted against the additional funding, turning the center into a glorified daycare, she couldn't see herself staying here.

Devon met them outside Café Bliss. “Sadie saw you, so we decided to meet you out here.”

Jenna noticed Cathy through the window. “Thanks, Devon. I appreciate it.”

“I won’t lie. I hope you two work things out, but I won’t interfere besides saying one thing. Your mother isn’t the same woman she once was.”

Jenna didn’t want to argue, and respected the man for not pushing too hard. She could see the love in his eyes for her mother, something she’d never really seen in her own father’s eyes. Had her mother been unhappy with her father? Had this man in front of her changed her mother? For the first time since she’d found out about her mother's lies, Jenna wanted to ask her mother about their past. But in the next breath, the anger resurfaced and she took Sadie’s hand. “Thank you. I’m sure I’ll see you at the Thanksgiving Feast.”

“I look forward to it. I’d love to watch Sadie again. She’s a sweet little girl.”

Sadie gave him a leg hug. “I had fun. Thake ou.”

Jenna wanted to tell Sadie how amazing it was that she said all that together, even if she didn’t quite say all the syllables, but she’d learned that sometimes calling attention to it made her shy away from trying. But based on Devon’s and Drew’s proud smiles, they’d realized it, too.

“Come on, princess. It’s time to get you and your mama home. I have to get to work.” He offered his hand to her and she took it. The sight of them walking hand in hand to the car brought tears to her eyes. She never thought a man would be in Sadie's life, and so soon after losing the one that should have been there. She shook off the image. It was too soon to think about a man in her life. Perhaps it was too soon to go to the feast with him.

"I'll see you at the Thanksgiving Feast." Devon waved.

Sadie clapped. "Feast? Food? Thakesgiving!"

Nope, Jenna wasn't getting out of that now.

She opened the rear door and reached into the backseat, but Drew was already strapping Sadie into her car seat. "Yep. If it's okay with you, I'll be going with you and your mama."

Sadie clapped again three times.

He closed the door and opened Jenna's. "I know what you were thinking three seconds after you asked, but now you can't get out of it." He winked. How did he always know what she was thinking? But it wasn't a recent development. He'd had that gift for as long as she could remember.

He backed the truck out of their space and headed back home. The thought of him dropping them off and leaving weighed on her heart, but she'd already set a date. She wouldn't ask him to do anything else before then. That would give her a chance to gather her thoughts, and hormones, in preparation for the feast.

They pulled into the driveway and Jenna lifted Sadie out of her car seat. "Got go." Sadie ran into the house and Jenna went after her.

“Not so fast," Drew called. "I’ve got something for you.”

Jenna was torn between helping Sadie and seeing what Drew had to show her.

“I think she’s got it. If not, she’ll call you.” He rummaged through a duffle bag he retrieved from the back seat and held out a small box to her.

“What’s this?”

“Since you kept that shirt all these years, I thought I’d show you what I’ve kept. Open it.”

Jenna leaned against the truck to steady herself before she opened the box. Inside, she found a necklace, his old class ring dangling from the chain.

“Your mother gave that back to me, along with a few other items after you left. I know it sounds silly, and that we can’t pick up where we left off, but I wanted you to have it.”

Jenna’s mind spun, unable to find words. “What else did she give back to you?”

As Drew rounded the truck to the other side, Jenna took several soothing breaths. Her eyes darted around to look for the right answer. Did she accept it? What did it mean? Her gaze settled on two books inside the duffle bag on the seat. The one on top had a picture of a child. She scooted the books around to read both titles. The top one was a book on raising a child with autism, and the other on how to show affection to a child with autism.

Her heart soared and her body fluttered with emotion. He came to stand beside her with a few items in his hand and she launched into him. Arms around his neck, feet off the ground, she kissed him, kissed him with all the passion of a seventeen-year-old girl in love. With a decade of missing him, and the rush of a newness between them.

CHAPTER FOURTEEN

For two days, Drew walked on a Jenna cloud. The woman had turned him upside-down and inside-out the way she always did. He couldn't wait to see her again. It was nearly a week until their date at the Thanksgiving Feast, but his wait was over thanks to the deadbolt lock Jenna desperately needed, sitting on the bench seat beside him. He'd showered, dressed and climbed into his truck before he even dialed the phone.

In only two rings, she answered, "Hi there."

"Hi. I wanted to stop by if that's okay. I have something that I wanted to take care of at the house. Would now work?"

"Sure."

"Great. See you in a few." He drove to her house and pulled into the driveway. He knew Jenna was worried about Sadie getting out of the house or answering the front door to strangers. He just hoped his solution did the trick.

Sadie ran out the front door and he captured her. "Hey, you. Where do you think you're going?"

"See you!" Sadie tightened her little arms around his neck and his heart soared, truly captured by the little one. She gave love so freely.

Jenna raced out. “Sadie, what am I going to do with you?”

“I might have a temporary solution for that.” He held up the plastic bag with the lock inside. “I thought we could secure the front door with this key lock. You can keep the key over the door where Sadie can’t reach it. It’s temporary, though. If you’re okay with it, I’m going to have an alarm system installed that’ll at least alert you if she tries to get out of the house at night or while you're busy doing something else. I figured you’d need it before school started anyway. From my limited knowledge, and from what I’ve seen of Mr. Rogers’s child, you’re going to need the alarm.”

Jenna took Sadie from him and they walked up to the front porch. “That's such a relief, but I can’t ask you to pay for it.”

“Don’t worry. One of your new client’s father is donating his time and giving all the parts at cost. He owns a security company.”

Jenna sat Sadie down inside and closed the front door. His old class ring swung on a chain around her neck. He captured it. “Looks good on you.”

She nodded. “I agree.”

Sadie skipped into the room next to the kitchen.

He retrieved the knife from his duffle and opened the plastic cover of the deadbolt. “Hey, I’d kind of like to know what elicited that kiss, so I can repeat it.”

She snuggled into him. “It might sound silly.”

“Silly is okay, as long as I can win another kiss like that one.” His toes still twitched at the thought of her taking hold of him and laying one on him before he even knew what was coming.

"Well, I saw the books in your duffle."

The muscles in his arms tightened. "I hope you're not mad. I wanted to make sure I didn't do anything that would upset Sadie."

Jenna pulled away, and a chill hit him. He dipped his head to hide his disappointment, but she grabbed his chin and turned him to face her.

"Are you kidding? That's the nicest thing a man has ever done for Sadie, and for me. I can't believe how well she's taken to you. She never even touched her father."

A sadness crept into Jenna's eyes and he wanted to chase it away. "You don't have to talk about it, but if you decide you want to, I'm here."

"That's it. You're here. He never was. Don't get me wrong, it was good in the beginning. But once Sadie was born, he withdrew. I guess he couldn't handle having a daughter that wasn't perfect."

"You know not all men are like that. I don't know your ex-husband, so I won't judge him. But the short time I've spent with Sadie, I can't imagine any father not being proud of that little girl. She's courageous and loving and beautiful, all qualities I love about her mother."

He held his breath, worried the word *love* would send her running from the room, but to his surprise she kissed him. His body welcomed the excitement and joy as they took over his senses. This kiss satisfied the longing, yet provoked more. He wanted to be with Jenna, forever. No other woman would ever make him happy the way she did. Lord knew he tried to find one, but there never was and never would be another woman for him than Jenna.

Sadie's skips sounded from behind, so he reluctantly took a step back from Jenna. His heart was pattering faster than Sadie's little feet.

He set to work installing the lock while Jenna and Sadie worked on some sort of puzzle in the front room. It took less than twenty minutes, and good thing since Sadie appeared at his side once more.

"Play with me?" Sadie snagged his hand led him to the front room where the toys were.

"How about I make us all some popcorn and we can watch a movie."

The thought of staying for hours filled him with warmth. "I'd love that."

Sadie released his hands and ran to the kitchen. "I help."

He followed them both into the back of the house and watched them get out popcorn kernels and saucepan. "Oh, good. I like the real stuff. I only make microwave popcorn at my place."

"Yuck." Sadie held her nose.

Jenna poured the popcorn in and covered the pot with a lid. "Sadie doesn't like microwave popcorn."

"I'll make note of that. Hey, do you need help unpacking these boxes. I don't mind helping set up some stuff tomorrow after work."

"We'd love that, but those couple of boxes on top are for Maverick. He'll be coming by on Saturday to fix the electrical."

Drew eyed the small appliance plugs all stuck into the one outlet. “I guess he didn’t think about kitchen outlets when he renovated. He probably never cooked here.”

Jenna shook the pot. “That’s what he said.”

“I’ll be glad when he gets that worked out. What else needs to be done? I’m working tomorrow and Friday, but I have good news.”

“What’s that?”

“Jimmy said that I can have the night off for the Thanksgiving Feast. We have a new guy that’ll be on duty. Jimmy and I will both be on call, but we’ll cover the feast in plain clothes.”

Jenna poured the popped corn into a large bowl Sadie was holding up for her. “Too bad. I was looking forward to seeing you in uniform.”

“Then I guess I’ll have to stop by tomorrow after work. That is, if that’s okay with Sadie.”

“Aha, aha, aha.” Sadie walked flatfooted over to the couch, balancing the large bowl between her arms.

“Hmm, interesting.” Jenna eyed Sadie.

“What?”

She laughed. “Nothing, just the therapist inside me thinking of new modalities. I guess I better be careful. I don’t want to turn my daughter into a Freudian child for my scientific curiosity.”

“I doubt we need to be concerned with that. I can tell how much you love your daughter. But then, what’s not to love.”

Jenna slid her hand into the crook of his arm and they settled onto the couch. Sadie climbed up, popcorn spilling over the sides of the large bowl, and promptly wiggled her way in between them.

"What are we watching?" he asked.

"*Lilo and Stitch.*"

He wrapped his arm around Sadie and rested his hand on Jenna's neck, who leaned into his touch. "What's it about?"

"You've never seen *Lilo and Stitch*?" Jenna asked.

He chuckled. "I'm afraid not."

"Well, Sadie, I think we'll have to watch the whole thing. Guess you can stay up late tonight."

"Yay, yay, yay" Sadie balanced the large bowl in her lap and shoved a hand full of popcorn into her mouth. After several chews, she said, "*Ohana* means family."

Jenna patted her head. "That's right, honey."

They snuggled under a large blanket and Jenna turned off the side lamp. It was dark and cozy, like when they used to watch movies on her couch at night. Of course, they'd watched old horror flicks back then. Now they were watching a kid's flick. It didn't matter though, he still had Jenna, almost alone in the dark.

By the end of the movie, the popcorn bowl was empty, Sadie slept, and he knew what *Ohana* meant. "That was a great movie," he whispered.

Jenna carefully rose and reached for Sadie, but he lifted the little girl and carried her upstairs to bed. Watching Jenna tuck her in, he made note of which stuffed animals occupied space on the bed and which night light she left on.

After he kissed Sadie on the head, he made his way downstairs, knowing this would be goodnight. Part of him wanted to never leave, but he knew she still needed time.

Her phone on the hallway table buzzed and he noticed five missed calls. "Is that your mother?"

"I'm afraid so." Jenna sighed.

"You know, I'm still mad at her, too, but she is your mother. Someday you'll have to speak to her again."

"I know, but right now I'm trying to remember who I am and not what failures I've made in my life. My mother was married to my father until he passed," she said, her voice hitching a little with sadness.

He couldn't help but reach out to comfort her. "I know. They were married a long time."

"My mother believes that marriage should never end. That once you marry someone, it's a lifetime commitment. She doesn't understand how hard I tried to make it work. If he would've tried at all, I know I could have stuck it out longer."

"Stuck it out? That doesn't sound like a good marriage. Divorce happens. I know it's sad, and I know if I was to get married I'd do everything I could to make it work. I'd be in a hundred percent, but it takes two. If for some reason the marriage reached a point where we were both unhappy, I wouldn't torture my wife. That being said, I wouldn't throw in the towel at the first sign of trouble either."

Jenna ran her thumb back and forth over his hand, distracting him.

"I believe you." Jenna let him go, retrieved the key, and unlocked the front door. "Thanks for doing this. I can actually take a shower now and not worry about

Sadie running out the front door. I'm not sure why she never goes out the back, but if there's one thing about Sadie, she's consistent."

He stood in the doorway with heavy feet. "She's amazing, just like her mother."

She squeezed his hand but didn't kiss him goodnight.

"Don't worry. Everything's going to work out. You're going to get the money and support of the county. Your daughter's going to continue growing and I'm going to be here if you need anything."

Jenna squeezed his hand again, and he noticed the tears in her eyes. "I don't deserve you. I left because I was scared of forever. "

His heart cracked, yet it bled hope. "What are you talking about? You left because your mother lied to you."

She took a stuttered breath. "Did I?"

"Let me guess. This came from Cathy?"

"No, Judy told me to analyze why I really left, why I didn't face you."

He forced himself to remain calm. Hearing she left because her mother lied was something he could get over, but leaving because she decided he wasn't the right one would demolish him. "What are you saying?"

Jenna wiped the tears from her eyes. "I don't know. That's what I'm saying. Maybe Judy was right. You told me to be honest. And honestly, I don't know if I left because of what my mother said. Did I leave because I wanted more and I used what happened as an excuse to leave, or did I truly believe it? I don't know the answer and you deserve better than that."

He stepped back and raked his hand through his hair. "You're right. I do."

CHAPTER FIFTEEN

Jenna pulled into the cemetery parking lot but couldn't manage to open the car door. Instead, she prolonged her conversation with Devon on the other end of the phone. "Thank you so much for staying with Sadie while I ran a few errands. You're a life saver. I'll be home in twenty minutes."

"Don't worry at all. We're having fun playing dolls. I haven't done this since my daughter was a little girl. Take your time. We'll see you soon. I've got to go. Sadie wants me to braid her hair and I need two hands for that."

Jenna reluctantly hit *end* on the cell phone. She was thankful Devon had offered to stay with her daughter and to not mention her mother. She didn't have many people to watch Sadie, and this was something she had to do alone. It would distress Sadie too much to see Jenna upset.

She grasped the door handle and shoved it open. If only she had Drew at her side, holding her hand. The way he had the day of her father's burial. It had been so long ago, yet the pain still felt so raw.

With fresh flowers in hand, she walked along the

narrow path to the row with her father's gravestone. Her hands shook and her mouth went dry. When she reached his plot, she discovered dying flowers, probably a week or so old, resting on the stone. Was her mother still visiting his grave? She knelt and moved the wilting flowers over and replaced them with the fresh ones.

She cleared her throat and pulled a tissue from her pocket, already feeling a lump in her throat. "Hi, Daddy. I'm sorry it's been so long. I've been away from Creekside for over a decade. You probably don't know, but Mama lied to me and I left because I thought Drew had cheated on me." She laughed, a little tension easing from her shoulders. "You'd probably be happy about that. You said Drew wasn't good enough for me. Actually, you didn't think any boy was good enough for me."

She wiped her sweaty palms down her jeans and clasped her hands on her thighs. "Oh, Daddy, I don't know what to do. I'm so confused. I'm a grown woman and I'm still spinning out of control. I'm afraid my life's been that way for so long I'm not sure how to stop it, but I have to for Sadie." She twisted the tissue in her hands. "Oh, right. You may not even know who Sadie is. I'm not sure Mama told you, but I have an amazing little girl. You'd adore her. I wish you were here to play with her." Her voice cracked with emotions and guilt. Why had she let Devon come over to watch Sadie? It felt like such a betrayal to her own father.

"Anyway, I wish you were here. I miss you so much. I miss our talks and our games, even if you did cheat at backgammon all the time. I miss your laugh and your gentle goodnight kisses on my forehead. I miss everything about you. I thought after all these years the pain would hurt less, but it doesn't." She broke down and cried. Cried for the lost years, for the changes in her family, for the broken home she'd left behind, and for the mistakes she was still making.

She pressed her palm to the stone, wishing she could feel his touch. "I thought I could do this." Resting her forehead on her hand, she whispered, "What should I do, Daddy? I need you to give me advice the way you used to when I was younger. What should I do about Drew? If I love him, why did I leave? Why can't I commit to him now? I want to, but I can't. I just can't. What's wrong with me?"

She heaved sobbing breaths, thankful no one was in the cemetery to witness her hysterics. Her entire body ached and she wanted to crawl into the grave by her father's side and go to sleep, but she couldn't. Sadie needed her. No matter what happened with the center, or her mother, or Drew, she needed to be there for Sadie. To hold her, read her stories, love her, and give her everything she needed.

Jenna sat there for several minutes, willing herself to feel her father's presence. "I miss you, Daddy, but I need to go. I need to get back to Sadie." She stood, kissed her hand then pressed it to his gravestone. "I'm going to be strong now, and it won't take me another ten years to return. I'll visit more often, I promise."

She walked to the end of the line of gravestones and pulled another tissue from her pocket before heading toward the parking lot. At the edge of the cemetery, she spotted a Sweetwater County Sheriff car, but she couldn't see who was inside. Before she could make her way to the bottom of the hill, it left. She reached for her phone, but changed her mind and left it in her pocket. If it was him, he obviously didn't want to see her, and she wasn't ready to face him. Not until she knew the answer to why she had left all those years ago, even if it meant losing him forever.

***

Drew parked outside J&L Antiques to work on some files, but he couldn't concentrate. What was Jenna doing at the cemetery alone? He didn't like her going out there by herself. He would've gone with her, but she didn't want that. She didn't want him. He pounded his steering wheel twice and wished he knew what to do to make her see they belonged together. He couldn't go through losing her again.

Tap. Tap.

He glanced up to see James standing outside with his coat wrapped tight around himself. "You okay in there?"

Drew rolled down the window. "Yeah, I'm fine. Sorry about that. It's just been a frustrating day."

"Not a problem. We all have those moments. Would you like a cup of coffee? I hear police officers drink free at Café Bliss. Heck, I bet she'll give me a free cup for bringing you inside." James lowered to eye level.

"I can't. I've got some work to finish up then I'm

heading home for the afternoon. I had an early shift today. Thought I'd hit the gym, or go for a run or something then get to sleep early."

"I'd offer to run with you, but I wouldn't be able to keep up. I've seen you fly by the shop before."

Drew chuckled. "Only on days when I'm frustrated, so yep, you might see that today."

James rested his hand on the car door. "You know, I'm here if you ever want to talk. I know your parents are gone, and Jimmy's probably busy with the baby coming and all."

"It's okay. I'm used to handling things on my own. My father disappeared early on and my mother checked out not long after."

"Yeah, but not for a lack of you trying to help her. Judy told me you were always trying to save people."

Drew shook his head. "I'm an officer, it's my job."

James eyed Judy inside the antique store then turned back to Drew. "Yes, but why did you become an officer? From what I hear, you struggled with taking care of your mother for years, but eventually she passed."

"I think you were misinformed. My father beat her and then left. After that, she became a drunk. She died from alcohol poisoning."

"Yes, that's what I was told. And that's why you became an officer? To save people? You know you can't save Jenna."

Drew snapped his head to the side. If this was Jimmy he'd tell him to butt out, but he couldn't disrespect James. "I'm guessing Judy sent you out here for a man-to-man talk. I know you're a famous psychologist, but you don't know everything about Jenna and me. I'm not trying to save her from anything."

"Aren't you? You've been holding her hand since she came back to town, helping her with Sadie, helping her with the center, helping her with things around the house. For years, you helped Jessica, but now she's leaving. You know, you can't save everyone. You need to let some people work through things on their own."

"Cathy got to you, huh? She's been trying to keep us apart since we were kids."

James held up a hand. "No, I'm just saying don't give up on Jenna just because she needs space to figure things out on her own. She's an independent girl. If she pushed you away, it doesn't mean she doesn't want to be with you. It's just...you can't fix her."

He tightened his grasp on the steering wheel, squeezing the molded material until his hands fatigued. He had no release for his frustration. He sighed. "She said she didn't know why she left, or if she wanted to be with me now."

James pressed his lips together and patted Drew's shoulder. "I know that's gotta sting, but sometimes people push you away in hopes of protecting you. It can take time for them to work things out."

"I get that, but I've waited over ten years already. How much longer should I wait?"

James eyed Judy through the window again. "I waited over forty and it was worth every minute."

CHAPTER SIXTEEN

Jenna glanced at her phone once more, but still no calls. What did she expect with the way she'd pushed her mother and Drew away? She glanced at the clock on the wall. With about an hour until Sadie woke from her nap, Jenna went through the kitchen, out the back door to the shed, and found the pots of flowers she'd picked up yesterday. This was good, a chance for some quiet time.

Her phone buzzed. She answered it but knocked an old terracotta pot off a shelf with her elbow in the process. It smashed to the ground with a loud crash. Sighing, she hit *talk* and said, "Hello?"

"Hi, hon. Sounds like you're expecting a call," Judy's voice, a pleasant tone with southern charm, filled the emptiness in the world around her.

She sighed again. "No. Not at all."

"You okay? Do you need something?"

"No, I'm good. I just knocked a planter off and broke it. No big deal." She scooped up the shards and tossed them into the trashcan. "What can I do for you?"

"Nothing, dear. I wanted to see how you were doing. James ran into our friend yesterday and he wasn't looking too good."

"Drew?" She had to fight the miserable guilt twisting and turning her into a frenzy of confusion.

"Yes. He said something that made me think you needed a friend to talk to about what happened with your mother and how you've been feeling."

Judy had always been like a second mom to her, even when she didn't want it. This time, she welcomed the offer. "Judy, I'm so confused. I wanted space so I could think. I don't want to hurt Drew again, but...I don't understand, though."

"Don't understand what?"

"Why don't I miss my own husband after the divorce, yet I've missed Drew ever since I left Creekside? Don't get me wrong. I wasn't pining for him while married to another man, but I chose to leave. I know now that you were right about that. If I'm such a fighter, why'd I run off thinking he'd been with Jessica? Yes, it hurt. Just the words made me want to drive off a cliff." She retrieved some of the flowers and a small spade then went to the front flowerbed and dropped to her knees.

"So, you want to be with Drew but you're scared you'll walk out on him again?"

Jenna dug a hole in the ground with more vigor than it required. Soil flew out in clumps at her side. "Yes, but the selfish side of me wants him here with me now. He's only been gone a few days and I ache to see him."

"What's holding you back then? Is he not good with Sadie? He's been a bachelor for a long time."

"Actually, he's amazing with Sadie. He's even been

researching how to relate to her better with her unique needs. He's carried her to bed, pushed her on the swing, held her while she watched a movie. He's been amazing."

"It sounds like you still care for him deeply. And he still cares for you, too."

"I don't know. I mean, he hasn't called for two days. The Thanksgiving Feast is tomorrow, and I don't even know if we're still going together. Sadie will be so disappointed."

"She will? Or you will?"

Jenna pulled flowers from their container and plopped them in the hole. Covering the roots with dirt, she patted it down gently. "I'd be disappointed, too," she admitted.

"Well, if you know you still care about him, why don't you call him and find out if you're still going?"

Jenna shrugged before she even realized Judy couldn't see her. "I don't know."

"I think when you figure that out, you'll know if it'll work between you two." Judy cleared her throat. "Um, there's one more reason I called and I fear I'm running out of time, so I'll just spit it out. Your mother is on her way over. Try to talk to her, if for no other reason than to tell her how you feel. She's tougher than you think. She can take it."

Jenna moved to the other side of the flower bed and planted a few more bunches. "Fine, but if they find my mother buried with these flowers later, I didn't do it."

Judy laughed. "That's the Jenna spunk I remember."

She hung up the phone, gathered her tools, and

headed for the back of the house to plant a few more flowers. It was probably too late in the season, but she wanted the center to be inviting to the children during opening week. If there was an opening.

She hadn't even started painting the walls, but she'd get that done after she knew for sure she'd be backed by the board on Monday. Her stomach rolled at the thought of the decision. It all rested on county politics now.

Her mother's car rolled by and Jenna heard it pull into the driveway out front. The sound of the engine cutting off made her mouth go dry. She brushed the dirt from her pants and readied herself for the fight.

The sound of steps over grass and snapping of twigs announced her mother's path to the backyard. Her mother rounded the corner, her hands clasped in front of her. "Hi, Jenna."

They stood for a moment, staring at each other before Cathy stepped closer. "I know I told you I'd stay away, but I just can't any longer."

Jenna dropped her tools to the ground and removed her gloves. "So talk."

"Don't you think we should go inside?"

Jenna glanced at a passing car and knew this would be big gossip for the town if they stayed out here. "Fine, but Sadie's asleep and I don't want to wake her."

Cathy rubbed her hands together. "I understand. I promise this will be a cordial visit."

Jenna entered the kitchen and flipped on the coffee pot, a habit of southern hospitality more than wanting to make her mother feel welcome.

Cathy remained close to the back door, as if she might need to run for her life at any moment. Smart woman. "Listen, I know you hate me. I deserve it, and I'm not going to deny that I did something horrible to my own daughter. I'm not asking you to forgive me. I just want you to say what you've been holding in these past few days. I'd rather hear the truth than live in silence any longer. Tell me you hate me, that I ruined your life, that you'll spend the rest of your days plotting my demise."

Jenna rubbed the back of her neck, trying to relieve the stiffness. "I see the new and improved Cathy Mitchell West still hasn't lost her gift for drama."

"New and improved? What does that mean?"

Jenna huffed. "Oh, please, Mama. Everyone can see it. You've gone from stay-at-home mom, who catered to Daddy and wore kitty sweatshirts, to this new woman in leggings and boots. You're skinny and have a new man. Did you just live that way all those years because you had to stay married to Dad? Does it make you a good woman because you stayed with him even if he didn't make you happy because you had kids and that was the right thing to do? Were you stuck with him longer because I was a surprise baby? Is that why you hate me, Mama, because I ruined your life?"

Her mother's mouth fell open. "Jenna, where is this coming from?"

Jenna crossed her arms over her chest. "I know I was an accident. I mean, I came along nine years after Jared. You've resented me my entire life because I ruined your exit plan. You wouldn't leave Daddy, not while there were still kids at home, so you were miserable. You've judged me since I was a young girl, telling me how I was sinning for being in love with Drew and how I needed a better life outside of Creekside. Was that really why you sent me away? Or was it so you could move on with your life? To a man that was better than Dad. Did you want me out of the way?"

Cathy gasped. "You were never a mistake. A surprise, yes. An amazing, wonderful surprise. Your dad and I were thrilled when we found out we were having you. We'd tried for years and then gave up. When we got pregnant with you, it was like a miracle. And I didn't stay with your father because of you kids. I loved your father. Yes, it is a different kind of love, but your dad was special to me and I miss him every day. Devon is different—passionate, romantic, and loving—but that doesn't change the relationship I had with your dad."

Jenna huffed. "Then what was it, Mama? You said you didn't want me to end up like you. You didn't want me to be unhappily married, living in a small town watching life go by. That doesn't sound like a woman who was happy with her family life. Well, news flash, Mama. I was unhappily married in a city, where I was more alone than I had ever felt in Creekside." Hatred coursed through her, but she wasn't sure who she hated more, her mother or herself.

Cathy dabbed the light sweat from her brow with a tissue. "Are you upset that I remarried? I tried to talk to you before we did, but you wouldn't come to the wedding."

Jenna gripped her hair, wanting to pull the memories of her father's death from her mind. "I don't know. Maybe, but in the same breath I'm glad you're happy. I'm glad Devon treats you well. You got your happily-ever-after with him, but I couldn't do it. I couldn't live with my husband any longer. I know you think I should go back and work things out with Shane, but I won't do that. I won't stay married to a man I don't love because that's what I'm supposed to do. He's not like Dad, he doesn't treat my daughter well. The price is too high."

Her mother reached out to her with a trembling hand, but she backed away. "I understand that now. I'm sorry I put you through this. I only wanted what was best for you, and you were dying here. I was terrified you were going to follow your daddy into that grave."

The floodgates of holding in all she wanted to say opened and it all spilled out. "You've tried to push me into doing things my entire life that didn't make me happy. I had to be on the cheerleading team because you always wanted to be a cheerleader. I had to leave Creekside because you always regretted staying. I'm not you, Mama. Drew made me happy and I wanted to stay."

"Jenna, you never obeyed a word I said growing up, and you know it. I'll take blame for many things, but you decided to be a cheerleader because Drew played football. I told you a lie that was unforgiveable, but I can't take the blame for every decision you ever made."

"Can't you? I never lived up to your expectations, Mama. Never."

"Jenna, stop!"

"No, you wanted to do this."

"Smoke!" Her mother pointed to the coffee pot.

Jenna smelled smoke then spun around to see flames spitting from the overused outlet. Her insides seared with fright. Her mother pushed her out of the way and grabbed the plugs, pulling them from the wall. Then she grabbed two towels and beat the wall until the flames disappeared back inside.

"Go get Sadie and call 9-1-1 to have them check the house," her mother ordered. Before Jenna could move, her mother turned, grabbed her chest and stumbled forward against the counter. "Jenna?"

"Mama!" She caught her mother before she hit the floor. "What's wrong?" Jenna's life flashed to the day she found her father on the ground. "No, no, no. I can't lose you, too. What's wrong?"

"Mama?" Sadie stepped into the kitchen, rubbing her eyes, then looked down at them on the floor.

Jenna snagged her phone from her pocket and dialed 9-1-1. "Stay with me, Mama."

Sadie squatted and began to hum, but Jenna couldn't focus on her needs for once. She had to get help. "Sadie, go sit on your bed."

Sadie didn't budge.

"911. What is your emergency?"

"I need an ambulance and a fire truck. Please hurry."

"Okay. I'm dispatching both, so try to stay calm. Can

you give me your address?"

Jenna swallowed hard and recited the address.

"They're on their way," the 911 operator said, "but I need you to remain on the line with me until they get there. Can you tell me what is going on?"

“My mother collapsed,” Jenna cried out.

“Is she awake?”

“No.”

“Did she do anything or say anything before she collapsed?”

Jenna held tight to her mother and rocked. “We were arguing and then she grabbed her chest and fell. She’s sweating.”

“Is it a cool, clammy kind of sweat?”

She held her hand to her mother’s damp face. “Yes. What is it? It’s not a heart attack, is it? Please tell me it’s not a heart attack.” Jenna tried to hold it together, but her nightmare was happening all over again. She couldn’t lose another parent.

Sirens sounded in the distance. Sadie curled up by her side and rocked, humming and crying. “It’s okay, honey. It’s okay.”

But it wasn’t okay.

CHAPTER SEVENTEEN

Drew heard the call over the radio and stomped on the gas pedal, racing over the bridge and down Main Street.

When he skidded to a stop in front of the house, a fireman was struggling with Jenna. She thrashed and screamed. "Mama! Mama!"

Sadie sat on the ground crying.

Jenna broke free from the fireman, and Drew caught her in his arms. "Are you hurt?"

"It's Mama. She's inside. I yelled at her...What have I done? It's all my fault. What will I do if she dies." Her body crumbled to the ground. He lifted her and settled her next to Sadie, who climbed into his lap and held tight to Jenna and him. Sadie continued to rock, her ears covered with her small hands, but her whimpering calmed.

The fireman stood close by, but Drew waved him away. "I've got them."

Paramedics lowered a gurney down the front porch steps to the ground and headed for the ambulance with Cathy. "Shh. She's going to be okay."

"Mama?"

He kept hold of her for a moment, not knowing Cathy's condition. "You stay here with Sadie. I'll check on her."

Jenna stood. "No, I need to. Stay with Sadie." She stumbled across the grass and stopped short of the paramedics maneuvering her mother across the front lawn. "Is she okay? Will she die?"

Drew could hear her trembling words, and wanted to do something, anything to make this better. This would destroy her. The guilt would eat her alive. *Dear Lord, don't let Cathy die.*

"We'll do our best, ma'am. We all know Cathy. She's done a lot for the fire department over the years. Let's get her to the hospital."

They wheeled Cathy by, and Drew buried Sadie's face in his chest. Jenna looked at him with pleading eyes. "Go. I've got Sadie. I'll meet you at the hospital."

As the ambulance pulled away, he lifted Sadie and she wrapped her little arms tight around his neck. His legs were shaky under him, but he managed to make it to the cruiser. He didn't have a car seat, so he sat in the back seat of the cruiser and held her tight while he dialed Judy.

"Hi, there. Did you talk to Jenna?" Judy asked.

"I'm afraid there's been an incident. Could you please come and get Sadie? I want to get to the hospital to be with Jenna, but I don't have a car seat."

"Be right there. I'm just leaving the shop."

"And Judy? Someone needs to call Devon. It's Cathy. She's being taken to the hospital. She collapsed."

There was a pause on the other end. "James will

take care of that. I'll be right there," Judy said, her voice tight with controlled emotion.

He rocked Sadie in his arms for what seemed like an eternity until Judy arrived. She parked on the street and opened her back door for him to set Sadie down, but she clung to him tighter.

"Sadie." He tried to pry her loose but she wouldn't budge. The little girl had been through too much, how could he possibly leave her? "I'll call Jimmy on the way to the hospital and have him take care of the cruiser. Can you take us both to the hospital?"

"Of course." Judy rounded the car and started the engine.

"Listen, honey," Drew said to Sadie. "I'm going to sit right next to you and I won't leave your side. Let's go see your mommy, okay?" Her thin arms loosened their grip, but her body shook. He strapped her in, removed his jacket, and covered her with it. "I think she might be in shock. We need to get her to the hospital and get her checked out."

"We'll be there in just a few minutes. How was Cathy and Jenna when you saw them?" Judy responded before she steered back onto the main road.

Drew's own body trembled at the memory. "Cathy was unresponsive and Jenna...Jenna will be destroyed if anything happens to her mother."

James's car appeared behind them by the time they reached the hospital. Devon jumped from the car before it even stopped and raced inside. Drew gathered Sadie into his arms and followed. "I need someone to check her out," he said the moment he reached the reception desk. "I think she's in shock." A nurse ran over, but Sadie wouldn't let go. "I think it'd be best if I stayed with her."

Devon stood at the counter. "Cathy West. She was just brought in. She's my wife."

Jenna rounded the corner, her face pale and blank. "Sadie? Is she okay?"

"Yes, but I'm getting her checked out. She's showing signs of shock. How's your mother?"

Jenna shook her head, her lip trembled. "I don't know. They haven't told me anything."

Devon joined them. "Jenna, where is she? What's going on? Is she..."

Jenna clutched his hand. "My mother is tough."

The nurse led them to a bed behind a curtain and Drew lowered Sadie's shaking body. "Your mommy's here, Sadie. Look."

"Mama." Sadie burst into tears. He moved and let Jenna hold her. He couldn't take his eyes off of them as they hugged and rocked together. He couldn't imagine life without them.

A doctor entered. "Officer, you'll have to wait until we're done checking them both before you can ask questions."

He'd forgotten all about the fact he was still on duty, but at that moment he didn't care. "I'm not here to ask questions. I'm with them."

"Are you family?"

He knew the drill, but still he was reluctant to leave them. He stepped back to the other side of the curtain. "No, I'll wait in the lobby."

"I'm going to check your lungs," the doctor said as he pressed the stethoscope to Sadie's back. She whimpered and snuggled deeper against Jenna.

The nurses and doctors raced around tending to the care of their patients as he walked back to the lobby. Monitors beeped, orders were given, the smell of cleaning fluid and lifesaving chemicals filled the air.

He caught a glimpse of Cathy, but a nurse shut the curtain before he could assess her condition. Another nurse firmly closed the door to the exam room. She acted like she knew him, but he couldn't focus long enough to process who she was. The door closed behind him and he placed a palm against the wall, willing this all to be okay. Cathy had to be okay, or Jenna would be consumed with guilt for the rest of her life. The stress of it all had taken its toll on Sadie, not to mention how distressed the little girl would be should Jenna suffer the loss of another parent. He'd only known her for a short while, but based on his research and what Jenna had said, that kind of stress could cause her to regress.

He leaned his head against the cool wall. Worst of all, he could lose Jenna forever this time.

A hand settled on his shoulder. "I'm able to go back with them. I know the chief cardiac surgeon here and he pulled some strings. I'll report back as soon as I discover anything," James said, his voice soothing, the same tone he probably used with his psych patients.

"What happened?"

James patted his shoulder. "I don't know for sure, but the paramedics told me there was a kitchen fire and then Cathy collapsed after putting it out."

He swung around to face James. "Kitchen fire? How bad?"

"Minor from what I understand."

Drew fisted his hands. "I should've fixed that. I knew that circuit was overloaded."

"It wasn't your fault. It could have been a grease fire, or something else. I don't know," James said.

"Or was it? I've got to know."

James quirked his head, but Drew didn't give him the opportunity to say anything. He spotted one of the firefighters, Ben, from the scene at the front desk. Drew adjusted his equipment belt and approached Ben. "Do we know yet how the fire started?"

"We'll have to wait for the official report, I'd only be speculating."

"Understood. But best guess. Was this arson, or accidental?" Drew fought for his professional composure.

"You can relax. I don't think anyone intended to burn down the center. The fire started in the kitchen. The old wiring couldn't handle the load. I'm not saying anything officially, but the fire appeared to have started at an outlet in the kitchen, so no need to start knocking on doors yet."

He had no doubt what Ben said was true. He'd known the appliances were too much for the circuit and didn't do anything about it.

He spun on his heels and walked around the waiting room chairs, not sure where to go. James stepped into his path and held up one hand. "What's going on? You look like you've just been court-martialed."

"I wish. The fire...it's my fault. I guess you were right. I did want to protect Jenna and Sadie, but I failed."

CHAPTER EIGHTEEN

Jenna cuddled with Sadie on the hospital bed. After sedation, she had finally calmed and fallen asleep. The hospital was dark, quiet, and unnerving, as if death patrolled the halls. Had it come for her mother?

The staff had moved them to a room to keep Sadie overnight for observation. The smell of disinfectant made Jenna's stomach roll. She wanted out, away from the reminders of her father's last days. She sniffled but didn't have the energy to keep crying.

Knock, knock.

The door opened and Judy appeared in the doorway. "Hi, darling. How you holding up? I'm sorry it's taken me so long to come see you."

Jenna had to fight her urge to jump out of bed and shake Judy for information. "Please, is there any news about my mother?"

"Yes, that's why I'm here. I would've been here sooner but someone had to calm your mother down. That's the good news. She's awake and doing well."

Relief flooded Jenna with soothing calm. "Thank God." Judy's heels clicked closer to the bed and after several deep inhales of happy relief she paused. "Wait, you said *good news*. What's the bad news?"

"That your mother's awake and giving the nurses and doctors hell. Devon's with her now. That man looks like he's about to collapse himself. I'll tell you one thing, she is his entire world."

Jenna smiled, genuine happiness flooding into her. "I'm glad." Then guilt seeped in. How could she have been so mean? "I was too harsh. I'm happy my mother found someone, but..." She sighed and leaned her head back against the small, paper-covered pillow.

"But you feel like you're betraying your dad? I get it. You two were so close. I think sometimes your mother was jealous of how close you two were. He never publicly showed affection to Cathy the way he did to you, but she was okay with that. She was happy with him. Now, she's showered with love and affection and it's changed her, but even now, I swear she'd give Devon up for you if you asked. We spoke the other day and she was convinced you hated her because she betrayed your dad."

Jenna bowed her head. "I did, or I thought I did. I think I felt more guilty about liking Devon and wanting to move on with my life here in Creekside when my dad's not here. It feels wrong."

"It's okay to feel those things, but your father loved you and your mother. I can tell you he would be happy for you both. He wouldn't want you to feel guilty." Judy clasped her hand. "Jenna, it's okay to continue living."

Freed from the anger and bitterness, she tried to process all the feelings she'd been keeping at a distance all these years. "My mother might be wrong on many things and have made her share of mistakes, but she's still my mother. The way she attacked that fire, I knew she'd give her life to protect me, just as I would my daughter."

Judy sat on the edge of the bed. "I'm so relieved to hear you say that. I know you're mother can be difficult, but she does things sometimes out of misguided love."

The monitor beeped on Sadie's cuff and inflated around her little arm, but she didn't stir.

"Poor little thing. She's got to be so upset." Judy swiped hair from Sadie's forehead with a gentle touch.

Jenna nodded. "I don't want her to feel upset at my pain anymore. I love her, and she deserves better. It's time for me to let it go and move on with my life. Maybe the center wasn't meant to be."

"You know, even if that's what happens it doesn't mean you have to leave Creekside again. You have family and friends here that will help. I know you're tough and you can handle anything that comes your way, you got that from your mama, but it never hurts to ask for help. We all would much rather help than see you leave. That would truly be a loss to this town."

Jenna squeezed Judy's hands. "Thank you. I don't know what I'd do without you. You've been there my entire life."

Judy stood and eyed Sadie. "As a grandmother, I can tell you without a doubt that Cathy loves this little girl more than anything. We had to stop her from driving up north to punch your ex-husband when she found out he wanted to put Sadie into an institution."

"Really? I thought she didn't approve of me getting a divorce."

Judy chuckled. "You two never did communicate well. I always felt like a translator. Well, good thing I'm here because you couldn't be more wrong. Cathy's thrilled you're here. She loves that granddaughter of hers, feels responsible for your bad marriage, and is so happy you had the strength to get out. She hopes you'll find happiness in Sweetwater County with Drew, even if you never want to speak to her again. She even spoke to Devon about moving up to the mountains, away from Creekside, to let you enjoy it here without worrying about running into her."

"She did?"

Judy chuckled again. "She did. Your mama only wants what's best for you. Always has."

Jenna relaxed back into bed. "Can I speak to her?"

"In the morning. She's out right now from the sedative. I'll come by and stay with Sadie when Cathy wakes, okay?"

"Thank you. Wait, Judy. One more thing. Where's Drew?"

Judy sighed. "Last I heard he was blaming himself for the fire. He's not doing too well."

"Okay. Thank you."

The moment the door closed behind Judy, Jenna snagged her phone from the side table and dialed Drew. It rang once then went to voice mail. "I need to speak to you. Where are you?"

***

The night felt like an eternity of solitude, where Jenna was imprisoned in the world of her own thoughts.

In the early morning hours, Judy poked her head back into the room. "You awake, darling?"

Jenna stretched and slid from under Sadie. "Yes, she's still resting though. She hasn't stirred at all."

"She's gonna be okay. She's got a little of her mama and grandmama in her. Speaking of grandmama, your mother's awake."

Jenna nodded. "Good, I'd like to see her. Would you stay here with Sadie?"

"It would be my pleasure. She's in room 2408. James just went for a coffee run. He's gonna bring you back something, too."

Jenna stopped at the foot of Sadie's bed. "That would be great, thanks. Um, has anyone seen Drew?"

"Yes, James found him last night."

Jenna clutched the edge of the hospital bed. "Is he here?"

"No, James finally got him to go home. He said the poor guy looked beat."

"I see." Jenna didn't know what else to say, and Judy didn't push. "I'll be back soon. I don't want to leave Sadie for too long."

"I promise to have you paged if she wakes up."

"Thank you." Jenna made her way through the halls to her mother's room. Nurses passed by pushing medicine carts with a forced smile and tired eyes. She reached 2408 and took a steadying breath before knocking.

"Come in," Devon called.

She pushed the door open and found Devon at her mother's side. Her face was still pale.

"You're welcome to come in, but I'm going to ask that you remain calm." Devon hesitated, but moved from her mother's side.

"I'm not here to argue, I promise." The sight of her mother in the bed with tubes running from her arm shot her with fresh grief. Tears poured from her eyes and she stumbled to the bed. "Mama?"

Devon stood a few feet away. "I'm going to go get some fresh ice chips for you."

Cathy opened her arms, but Jenna carefully sat on the side of the bed and leaned into her. "Mama, I'm so sorry. The things I said...If I had lost you—"

"I'm fine. Your silly mama just had some sort of panic attack."

Devon paused at the door. "That's not entirely true. They're running tests, but it's possible she needs a stent in her heart."

Devon closed the door behind him, and Jenna lost it. She blubbered like a little girl with a skinned knee.

After several minutes, her mother patted her head. "Okay, now. That's enough. I'm good. I'm way to stubborn to die on you, so sit up. We need to talk about a few things." Her mother always did subscribe to the tough-love handbook. "First, you were right to be angry, and I deserve everything you said. Next, I assure you that you have never been an afterthought in my life. I loved you and wanted you from the first moment

I found out I was having another baby. Were you a few years after your brother? Of course, but no less precious to me. You were my baby girl, and I've always loved and admired you."

Jenna grabbed tissues from the tray table then wiped her eyes and blotted her nose. "I know, Mama, I just sometimes felt like I wasn't good enough."

Cathy chuckled. "Oh, honey, you were too good for me from the day you pranced into my room at the age of three and told me what real life was all about. And you never stopped giving me hell since."

Jenna lowered her head. "I know I wasn't always the easiest to deal with."

"I wouldn't trade a second of our life together for anything, honey. I love you, your brother, and your father. I'm afraid I was just trying to make sure you lived the life you deserved. I thought that you should go out and rule the world, and that Creekside would keep you stifled. After your father died, you lost that glimmer in your eyes. The one that showed the world you owned it. I saw you withering away and I wanted you to get out of this town because I thought you needed to find a new path. But I know what I did was horrible and wrong in so many ways."

"It was, Mama, but I realize now that what you said wasn't the only reason I left. I needed to leave."

Her mother scrooched up, but winced and clutched her chest. Jenna fluffed the pillows behind her and eased her back. "Is that better?"

"Yes, dear. Thank you. Now, why do you think you had to leave?"

Jenna shrugged. "I wish I knew. I love Drew. I've always loved him."

"And he's always loved you. I've never seen a man more head over heels for a girl before." Her mother patted the bed, directing Jenna to sit back down. "You know, when your father died, I was in my own world of pain and I never really saw how you were dealing. Your brother was already away and making his own way in life, but you and I were left here. I saw you pulling away from me, and Drew told me you were doing the same with him. He was worried about you, but all I could see was my daughter suffering. I knew you needed out of here, and you took it the first opportunity. Don't you see why you left?"

Jenna shook her head.

"You didn't leave because you didn't love Drew. Your heart was broken from your dad's death, and you didn't have enough left to share. You loved Drew too much."

Jenna inhaled a sharp breath. The ache she'd felt in her heart all this time wasn't from worrying about failing again or not wanting to rush into anything. It was because she loved Drew with all her heart, all her soul, and all her body. The deep-in-your-bones-can't-breathe-or-eat-at-the-thought-of-losing-them kind of love. She rubbed the stiffness in her chest and swallowed the fear. "You're right."

"Ha! That's a first." Cathy smiled and nudged her elbow into Jenna's arm. "Then what are you going to do about it?"

"I'll call him. I can't leave you and Sadie right now."

Her mama gave her that you-better-wise-up stare.

"I'm already on the mend and so is your daughter. From what I hear, that man of yours is in a world of pain, and I think it's about time you helped heal that heart."

Jenna hugged her mother around the neck then ran to the door. "I love you, Mama."

"I love you, too."

She nearly ran into Devon as she raced from the room. "Sorry, I have to go." She ran all the way back to Sadie's room, who still slept soundly. The nurse was checking her vitals.

"Do you know how much longer she'll be asleep?"

The nurse checked the chart. "Probably another few hours."

James entered, and handed her a coffee then sat down by Judy.

"James, can you take me to Drew? I need to find him." She had to talk to Drew, but it still frightened her to let Sadie wake up without her.

James stood and kissed Judy on the cheek. "It would be my pleasure."

They headed to the car. She'd finally tell Drew she loved him. She just prayed it wasn't too late.

CHAPTER NINETEEN

Drew ripped the socket from the wall and threw it across the room. The fire and smoke damage was less than he'd expected, but still, he'd failed to keep them safe despite the fact it was his job to protect those around him. He'd failed his mother, and now he'd failed Jenna and Sadie.

Footsteps sounded behind him, but he just wanted to be alone. "James, I don't want to talk anymore. I'm going to fix this then head home."

"Drew," Jenna said.

Her voice jolted him, and he turned to find her at the back door. The sunlight glowed around her like a halo.

"I've been looking for you everywhere. I need to talk to you." Jenna approached with a tentative step, her hands in her pockets and her lips tight.

He didn't want to hear what she had to say, fearing it was that she was leaving, or that she'd made up her mind they didn't belong together. For once, he'd be okay with her disappearing, if only temporary. "How is Cathy?" He gripped the damaged wall and yanked plaster out.

"She's as bossy as usual. As a matter of fact, she ordered me to come talk to you."

"Did she?" He tossed the drywall on the ground and grabbed another section. Did he want to know, or did he want her to leave so he'd never have to face her rejection.

Jenna's hand pressed to his back and he halted. "You need to listen to me. This wasn't your fault, even if the old outlet did cause the fire. You told me not to plug in too many things, remember? Besides, you're a policeman, not a firefighter. And even a superhero can't save everyone."

"It should've been taken care of immediately. It's an old house, despite all the renovations. It's not safe for you and Sadie to live here, or to let any children of Sweetwater attend an after-school program here."

"Maverick's going to call in an electrician to inspect the entire house. We'll make the necessary changes before the school opens. It's gonna take more than a little kitchen fire to drive me away."

He spun to face her. "You were right. You should go and do what makes you happy." Even if it meant never seeing her again, he couldn't stand to see her unhappy or in danger.

She clutched his arms. "Listen to me. Cathy's fine, I'm fine, Sadie's fine. If Sadie would've been hurt because of my stupidity, I don't know what I'd do. And as for my mother, I'm the one that put her in the hospital, not you." Her head lowered, her eyes settling on the tile floor. "I said horrible things to her. That's why she's in the hospital, not because of the fire." She sighed. “Maybe I was in over my head with all this, but I wanted to return to Creekside...to you, so bad I didn’t think about the consequences.”

“To me? I thought you’d realized it was a mistake, that you chose to leave me the last time because you weren’t sure how you felt about me.”

Jenna brushed hair behind her ear with a trembling hand. It was chilly and she wasn’t wearing a jacket. He wanted to warm her, to make her pain go away, but he couldn’t. Not any more. The price was too great to comfort her only to have to walk away in the end.

“That’s not why I left.” She took a long breath.

He rubbed his throbbing head. “I don’t understand.”

She gripped his arms and stared him down. “I didn’t leave because I didn’t love you enough. I left because I loved you too much,” Jenna said, her voice rising.

He broke free and backed away.

Jenna threw her hands up in the air. “Listen to me. When my father died, my entire life fell apart. You held me and told me it would be okay, and I tried to believe you, but I couldn’t. I didn’t realize it before, but losing the most important person in my life at the time had changed me. It made me never want to feel that kind of pain again. I should have talked to my mother, or to you more, but everywhere I went in town there was a reminder of my father and that he was gone. That I would never see him again, never feel his warmth. I knew I wasn’t strong enough to lose you, too.” Her voice cracked.

“You left because it was too hard to love me anymore?” He shuffled toward her until they stood toe to toe. “You didn’t leave because you wanted more out of life, because you wanted to live in a big city and marry a rich man and have some fancy career?”

“No, all I’ve ever truly wanted was to return home, to marry you, to be a family again in the one place in the world where I belong. I wouldn’t blame you if you hate me for all I’ve put you through. Trust me, if I could slap the eighteen-year-old me, I would.”

“You’re not...scared anymore?" Was she really ready to open her heart? He willed her answer to be *yes*, but could he trust she wouldn’t run away again?

Jenna placed her palm over his heart and captured his gaze. “I’m not scared anymore. None of this scares me. My daughter was distraught in the hospital. My mother nearly died, yet the thought of losing her woke me up. Made me realize how many years we’ve lost because I was scared. Drew, I don’t want to lose any more time, not even a minute. I want to live my life, and I want to live it with you.”

Multiple emotions, ranging from fear to elation, all roared through him, but he could only settle on one, the one he’d always known to be true. “I love you, Jenna. It’s always been you and only you.” He took her in his arms and kissed her with all the passion of yesterday, the love of today, and the promise of tomorrow.

CHAPTER TWENTY

The aroma of pumpkin bread, turkey, and stuffing filled the air. Jenna took a sip of her apple cider, enjoying the warmth of cinnamon as it slid down her throat. The large barn-like facility the town had built after she'd left was brimming with people. It was an amazing structure, a perfect place to have the Thanksgiving Feast. A long table, reaching from one end of the barn to the other, along with two more tables formed a large *U* shape. In the center of the space, she spotted the seat that once was set in honor of her father. This year the nameplate read *Frank Miller*.

Drew lead her through the crowd to the buffet table. She held tight to Sadie's hand, keeping an eye on her to see if the noise and lights were too overwhelming. As much as she loved the feast, she didn't want to stress Sadie out to the point of her developing night terrors.

They stood next to the food table. All the country home cooking made her stomach growl. Thank goodness the fiddler played loud enough it covered the noise.

Judy and several other women uncovered the various dishes, full of homemade, top-secret family recipes, and set out serving utensils. She hadn't had good home cooking for so long, she thought she'd just dig in right there.

"It's just how I remembered it." Jenna held tight to Drew and followed him to the back where Sadie ran over to other children playing on bales of hay.

"You know, I haven't attended one of these feasts since you left. I've worked it plenty, but I've usually done parking and crowd control outside. It's good to be here as a resident this year." Drew hurried over to stop a bale of hay from falling and keep Sadie from tumbling down.

Jenna joined them. "You can't always protect her."

"I can try." He set her down near two other little girls playing with dolls, and Sadie showed off her new green dress with white lace that he had bought her.

"You also need to stop spoiling her. She's going to become a brat." Jenna hip-bumped him.

Devon, her mother, and a young man and woman she didn't recognize made their way through the crowd to join them. Devon was like a human shield making sure no one bumped into his wife.

"Hi, Mama. I didn't expect you to make it. You sure you should be out?"

"That's what I told her, but you know how stubborn she can be," Devon said.

The young woman smacked him on the arm. "Calm down, Dad. Let her breathe."

"This bossy lady is my daughter, Becca, and this is Rusty Miller." Devon pointed.

Jenna shook both their hands. "It's nice to meet

you." She eyed the place of honor at the head table before returning her attention to Rusty. "I'm sorry for your loss."

Rusty held tight to Becca. "Thank you. My grandfather was a good man, even if he was a little stubborn."

Cathy slapped her thigh. "A little? Ha, the man could argue with a brick wall and win."

Jenna cringed at her mother's outburst about the young man's grandfather, but Rusty only nodded and smile. Becca took his hand. "We're gonna go visit with Rose and Marcus. They're only home from college for a few days. We'll catch ya later." They faded into the large crowd beyond Jenna's view.

"You should sit down." Devon ushered Cathy to some chairs.

Cathy sat but waved her hand at him. "Shush, and go get me some punch before you smother me."

Drew sat next to her mother. "I'll take good care of her. Jenna, would you mind getting me some more apple cider? I'd like to talk to your mother for a moment."

She wasn't sure she liked him and her mother being alone together, afraid an argument would have her mother relapsing, but Devon snagged her arm and headed to the beverage table before she could protest. They waited in line and the entire time Jenna kept her eyes on those two. "What do you think they are talking about?"

Devon shrugged. "It's *your* mother. You probably have a better idea. I know she's excited you've agreed to stay in Sweetwater County despite the possible outcome of the center."

"Yes, well, I hope I have a job still, or it'll be far more complicated to stay."

Devon scooped the ladle through the bowl of cider and poured some into her cup. "I wouldn't worry too much about it. According to Cathy, they're more worried about a lawsuit than your job. Rumor has it that Maverick sent a message to the board via email, informing them that an additional electrical inspection should have been completed prior to you moving into the house, and someone dropped the ball."

She held his cup up for him to pour some. "I don't want a job because they're scared I'm going to sue them. It wasn't their fault. It was an accident."

Devon smiled. "Small town politics. Trust your mother. She wrote the handbook on board manipulation. She makes things happen around here. Town gossip reports that not only are you going to receive the funds, but they're working with Riverbend to start a joint program. After you spoke to them about an intern, it turns out that Riverbend is in need of a facility also. It may require you being head of both, with staff under you, but I know you can handle it."

Jenna's pulse raced with excitement and fear, but it was good fear. "I don't know what to say, except that I'll work hard and make sure the kids are getting what they need."

"I know you will."

They made their way back to her mother and Drew. He had a strange look on his face, but her mother was beaming bright.

"What? I know that look. Both of you are up to something."

Drew took the cup from her hand and handed it to Devon. "You asked me by my truck one day what else I kept of ours, but I didn't get a chance to answer before you laid that kiss on me." He touched his class ring hanging from a chain around her neck.

She felt the heat in her cheeks and avoided eye contact with anyone but Drew.

"I wanted you to wear this like old times, but it wasn't the ring I really wanted to give you. Many years ago, I purchased a different kind of ring. It isn't much since I didn't have any money then, but I've kept it all these years." Taking both of her hands in his, he knelt down on one knee. "Jenna, your father wasn't here for me to ask, so I spoke to your mother and she gave her blessing." He removed an old box with pale white cloth around it from his pocket and opened it to reveal a small, shiny, diamond chip ring. "As I said, I bought this years ago, and I'd like to take you to pick out the ring of your choice, but I hope for now you'll accept this. I want to marry you and to be a father to Sadie. I know this is fast, but I've wanted this for so long. Will you marry me?"

Jenna felt tears run down her cheeks. She eyed the ring and fought her trembling lip so she could speak. All the fear was gone, replaced by hope and love.

"Well, are you going to answer the boy, or are you going to wait until I'm dead?" her mother asked.

Jenna shot her a look and Devon growled at her.

"What? Too soon?" Cathy chuckled. "Boy, you all are a sensitive bunch."

Jenna grasped the small box. She couldn't imagine him keeping it for over a decade. "I love you, Drew Walker. I've always loved you. It's not too soon. It's long overdue and the ring is perfect. Yes, I'll marry you."

The entire room clapped and they were flooded with their friends and neighbors as everyone came to offer their congratulations. Some she recognized, others she was yet to get to know. All of them were part of her town family. Sweetwater County, Tennessee, was, and always would be, the town where her heart and home belonged.

If you've enjoyed this story please take a second to write a review or tell a friend about what you've read.

For more information please visit
http://www.ciaraknight.com.
Or send her an email at:
ciara@ciaraknight.com

ABOUT THE AUTHOR

Ciara Knight is a USA Today and Amazon Bestselling author who writes 'A Little Edge and A Lot of Heart' that span the heat scales. Her popular sweet romance series, Sweetwater County (rated G), is a small town romance full of family trials, friendly competition, and community love. Also, there is a brand new sister series, Riverbend. The prequel novella is now available on all online retailers, and the first four books will release in 2016.

When not writing, she enjoys reading all types of fiction. Some great literary influences in her life include Edgar Allen Poe, Shakespeare, Francine Rivers and J K Rowling.

Her first love, besides her family, reading, and writing, is travel. She's backpacked through Europe, visited orphanages in China, and landed in a helicopter on a glacier in Alaska.

Ciara is extremely sociable and can be found at Facebook @ciaraknightwrites, Twitter @ciaratknight, Goodreads, Pinterest, and her website ciaraknight.com.

Made in the USA
Middletown, DE
06 December 2021

54494253R00104